THE RUNNER

Books by Cynthia Voigt

THE BAD GIRLS SERIES

Bad Girls

Bad, Badder, Baddest

It's Not Easy Being Bad

Bad Girls in Love

Bad Girls, Bad Girls, Whatcha Gonna Do?

THE TILLERMAN SERIES

Homecoming

Dicey's Song

A Solitary Blue

The Runner

Come a Stranger

Sons from Afar

Seventeen Against the Dealer

THE KINGDOM SERIES

Jackaroo

On Fortune's Wheel

The Wings of a Falcon

Elske

OTHER BOOKS

Building Blocks

The Callender Papers

David and Jonathan

Izzy, Willy-Nilly

Orfe

Tell Me if the Lovers Are Losers

Tree by Leaf

The Vandemark Mummy

When She Hollers

THE RUNNER

CYNTHIA VOIGT

ATHENEUM BOOKS FOR YOUNG READERS
New York London Toronto Sydney New Delhi

ATHENEUM BOOKS FOR YOUNG READERS
An imprint of Simon & Schuster Children's Publishing Division
1230 Avenue of the Americas, New York, New York 10020

Also available in an Atheneum Books for Young Readers hardcover edition
Book design by Debra Sfetsios-Conover
The text for this book is set in Baskerville.
Manufactured in the United States of America
First Atheneum Books for Young Readers paperback edition July 2012
2 4 6 8 10 9 7 5 3
The Library of Congress has cataloged the hardcover edition as follows:
Voigt, Cynthia.
The runner.
Summary: As a dedicated runner, a teenage boy has always managed to distance himself from other people until the experience of coaching one of his teammates on the track team gradually helps him see the value of giving and receiving.
ISBN 978-0-689-31069-0
[1. Runners (Sports)—Fiction. 2. Interpersonal relations—Fiction.] I. Title.
PZ7.V874Ru 1985
[Fic] 84-21663
ISBN 978-1-4424-5066-0 (hc)
ISBN 978-1-4424-2881-2 (pbk)

WITH
MANY THANKS,
TO MY MOTHER
&
FATHER

Runners
and track fans
will undoubtedly notice
that I have taken liberties
with the order of the sports year.
I hope they will, despite
this, permit me
the story.

THE RUNNER

1967

The time you won your town the race
We chaired you through the
marketplace.
Man and boys stood cheering by
As home we brought you, shoulder
high.

CHAPTER 1

Bullet was angry. He crashed his supper plate and milk glass down beside the sink and walked out of the kitchen.

Where did the old man think he got off?

On the back porch he pulled off the oxford shirt and khakis he'd put on for dinner, stripping down to the shorts and T-shirt he wore underneath. He was angry, good and angry. He was mad, good and mad. Bad and mad, bad mad . . . His feet picked up the rhythm of his anger.

He pounded down the path through the vegetable garden, heading for the water. He was PO'd, pissed off, he was royally pissed off, and he didn't care what they thought. He didn't give a royal fart for the two of them sitting at that table back in the kitchen. Bullet made his hands into fists, brought his knees up high and stomped his feet into the dirt of the path. The way the old man talked to him, it made him mad.

Where did he think he got off talking to him like that—as if he still thought he could make Bullet do anything. The guy was book smart but life stupid, trying to box Bullet in with— As if he could make him do anything.

If it came to a fight he knew he could whip the old man with one hand, with no hands the way he felt now, just hitting at the old guy with his head and kicking—and his teeth too. Bullet was seventeen, even if he didn't have the license to prove it, because he wasn't allowed to get a license; seventeen and he'd wear his hair any damned way he wanted to. Angry enough to rip tendons out of the old man's arms with his teeth if all of his other weapons were lost. And he could do it too. Only he couldn't, because there never was a real fight between them. Just these petty boxing-in orders. Well, he picked and chose what orders he'd follow, he'd learned a while back how to do that. It wasn't easy, that learning, but nobody said growing up wasn't going to hurt.

He came to the dock and stopped. His chest was heaving: he'd taken the quarter mile at a full run and that was stupid. Bad enough that he had to do his running on a full stomach—because his father wanted dinner at 5:30 exactly, and everybody he was feeding at the table to eat. Bullet couldn't do anything about that, but he knew better than to start out at full force. You were supposed to loosen up slowly, and now he'd have to rest before he started his evening run. This was his third year running cross-country, he shouldn't be making that kind of mistake. He stood at the end of the dock, listening to his heartbeat slow, letting his muscles ease down.

He was looking out over the water, but he felt the land stretching away behind him, flat, fertile fields marked off by tall, straggly loblollies and little stands of pines. The broad belt of marsh grass whispered under the wind, behind him, beside him. Through the soles of his sneakers he could feel the land, firm and deep, beneath him.

"Get your hair cut. You look effeminate," his father had said, his voice dry as harvested hay.

Bullet had just looked at him, but the old guy never looked at you, never looked you in the eye. Mostly, Bullet didn't answer his father. *I don't have to listen to this,* he said inside his head, at his father's face. *As long as I do my work, that's what you're entitled to and I work my tail off.*

"Effeminate means girlish," the sarcastic voice had said, as if Bullet didn't know that. The cold eyes had gone down to the other end of the table, where Bullet's mother sat. She didn't say anything, she never would anymore. The old man wanted to run things, and he wanted you to say something so he could knock you down with his answer and box you in tighter. If she said something, it wasn't her he'd try to knock down, it was Bullet, just the way he had with Johnny first, then with Liza. Driving them away, to drive them away. Bullet's mother sat there, her eyes dark and angry, her mouth still as stone.

Bullet had hooked his hair behind his ear and kept on eating.

"I want that hair cut tomorrow." His father gave the order.

If wishes were horses, Bullet answered inside his head with the old nursery rhyme, *beggars would ride.* The thought struck him as funny.

"Or I'll take the scissors to you myself."

No.

There was a wind blowing up from the south, blowing in thick, heavy air. Bullet didn't mind that. He never minded weather, even when the muggy summer air hung so close and humid you couldn't sweat into it. His eyes drifted out to the end of the dock—Johnny's boat was still there, still afloat. He wondered how many years it would be before the wood gave out to the weather and the thing just sank. His mother was the only one who ever took it out, and she bailed it too and scraped as much of the bottom as she could get to standing beside it in the shallow water. But she couldn't get it out of the water for the winter, didn't have time to caulk and paint the hull, never had any money, so she couldn't have it hauled at one of the boatyards. Too bad. Too bad the old man wouldn't let her get a driver's license either, because that meant the only way she could get around on her own was this sailboat. Which would, someday, sooner or later, just rot away.

He turned away from the little waves, blown over the top of the water under a September sky, and let the wind hit his back. He was about ready.

But before he could take off, he heard pattering footsteps and panting behind him, where the path came down to the shore from the marsh grasses. A cold nose touched his calf: "Get," he said without looking. "Get lost, OD."

The dog ignored the order. She stood wagging her tail, her brown eyes staring up at him, her tongue lolling out of her mouth. He turned around and raised a foot to kick at her. Liza's old dog—Florabella was what Liza tried to get them to call her. Bullet named her OD, for Old Dog—and because the dog was an overdose of Liza's stupid softheartedness. Liza found her one morning, just swimming out in the middle of the bay. Somebody had dumped a litter of puppies overboard—without even bothering to weight down the sack, apparently—and this one was just swimming away stupidly, putting off drowning. Liza and Johnny got her into the boat, and Johnny had gotten the old man's permission for Liza to keep the puppy. That was back in the days before the old man paid much attention to any of them, before Johnny started growing up and getting angry. Bullet couldn't have been more than four when Liza found OD. OD was really getting to be an old dog, thirteen was pretty old for a dog. She lived in the barn and Liza used to feed her and play with her—he guessed his mother might be feeding OD now, Liza had been gone for a few years. The only thing Liza left behind when she took off with Frank was this dog. Just like leaving something of herself behind, because the dog was about as stupid as Liza was.

When Bullet raised his foot, OD backed off. She crouched low to the ground and waved her tail to appease him, but she kept her stupid brown eyes on his face. He turned full around, raised his arms and roared at her. She backed off, fast, afraid, stopping where the path entered the marsh grass. The grass towered over her. She was no taller than a beagle, even though she was rounder, with long golden hair. He roared again, jumped twice at her King-Kong style, and she fled up the path. He fired off a couple of oyster shells at her rump, to keep her going.

Bullet wouldn't have minded a good hunting dog, a hound or a bird dog. But the old man would never let him. First it was, "You're too young to take the responsibility," then, "You're too old for pets." There was never any argument you could have with him. Unless you were Johnny, but if you were Johnny you would have been a carbon copy of the old man and Bullet didn't want to be that. His old man was a nothing, nothing but right answers and holding on to his precious farm.

Bullet bent down and straightened up, ten slow toe touches, breathing in deep and easy, getting his palms flat on the ground. *Hold on,* he said to himself. *Be fair*. The old man was bad enough as he was, there was no need to be unfair. The guy was a crack shot, for one thing. Every year he got his deer, as well as the quota of goose and duck. To watch his father bring down a deer was a treat. The old guy never hesitated, never took more than one shot.

And the old man knew about things, he'd learned a lot and remembered it. Science and mechanics and farming, but also history and what people long dead had said—he could answer just about any question you asked him. If you asked him a question. But he didn't listen to other answers, and it took Johnny years to figure that out, once Johnny had some answers of his own. Not Bullet, Bullet learned from watching the two of them, learned a lot. Johnny'd try his own answers, and at first the old man scared him and boxed him in with how much more he knew; but as Johnny grew up he got angry instead of scared. Bullet figured it out: little kids you could keep boxed in, so that was okay with the old man; but older kids could fight back and he couldn't take that. The more Johnny fought back the more his father boxed the rest of them in, and Momma too. Bullet learned that, fast and good, because nobody—he stood up straight, his arms wide, breathing air deep into his lungs—but nobody was going to get close to boxing him in. Nobody. No way. Not ever. He'd been his own man for years.

Bullet started on the run. Beginning in March, he ran his ten-mile course every evening. Up five miles along the shoreline, back five miles. Rain or sleet made no difference to him. He'd be out there in his shorts, T-shirt and sneakers. Cross-country took that kind of training. Bullet didn't have to train like this to win the races, but that wasn't what he was after, anyway, just winning. He had to train to keep getting better, to be as good as he could. And he was really good.

The course started off along the narrow beach, then cut inland—up over the eroded banks and fallen trees, through undergrowth, then back down to the muddy sand. Sometimes Bullet swerved inland to a field and pelted across it, his footing tested by the furrows with dried cornstalks like giant stubble, every footfall calculated. Sometimes he made short zigzagging spurts, ten yards up a beach, then five at the overgrown land's edge, testing the spring in his legs and his ability to get over obstacles, or through them.

You never knew what kind of land a cross-country course would cover. The disadvantage of training down on the eastern shore was that the land was so flat. The meets up north, or in the western part of the state, could be killers if you weren't used to working uphill. Cross-country was a killer anyway, but that was why Bullet liked it. Running around a cinder track, or even hurdling when they put jumps up at specified distances, you might as well be a horse, a trained horse going over the jumps they put out for you. But cross-country—he turned at the edge of a field where a pumpkin crop was ripening up and headed south again—cross-country was really tough. You had to be fast, but that was just the beginning. You had to have endurance, too, and quick reflexes. You were going to fall, you always did, but you had to get up fast and keep going. And smart, you had to be able to look at what lay ahead and get ready for it, you had to run smart.

Somewhere between the eighth and ninth mile, he began to feel the work his muscles were doing. From then on, he ran on strength alone, keeping up the steady pace, just not paying any attention to what his body was trying to say to him. After a little while he didn't feel anything. He'd run past it, run through it, and his body got back to the work he intended it to do. A year ago, Bullet would have hit that point at around five miles—hit it and gutted his way through it.

For the last quarter mile he ran along the flat beach. That was the way most cross-country courses were, too, a flat run at the end. Bullet sprinted, driving his feet into the wet sand, pumping his arms faster, to force the faster rhythm on his legs.

Back at the dock again he stood straight.

He wanted to fall down onto the boards—he could have thrown up his whole supper without any trouble at all, lots of guys did just that at the end of every race. But Bullet stood straight and locked his throat tight. His chest heaved, he couldn't even focus his eyes on anything, as if a film of blood spread over his retinas. He stood straight, arms loose at his sides, his shaking legs holding him firm. Every muscle in his body had been used and felt it.

Sweat poured down his back and legs, stung in his eyes, soaked his armpits. He liked that smell of sweat.

When his vision cleared, he took a look at the sun. His time was okay. He looked at the water and wanted to fall into it, but because he wanted to, he waited. He knew he could do that to himself, for himself; he'd learned that, too.

The sun hung red, just above the watery horizon—as if it were being sucked down into the water. The water reflected the cloudless gray-blue of the sky. When he no longer needed to, Bullet allowed himself to go swimming. The tide was up. Wind slapped the waves against the sides of Johnny's boat. A single star burned low above the horizon, obscured by the brightness of the sun. Bullet did a shallow dive off the end of the dock, then splashed around for a while. This late in the year you didn't have to worry much about jellyfish. Water soaked his clothes and shoes and all of his skin. He hauled himself back up onto the dock and sat there, looking out. His sneakers were heavy. His hair was plastered onto his forehead and clammy down the back of his neck.

It wasn't even as if his hair was that long, only halfway down his neck, and it looked good, thick and dark brown like his mother's. Some of the people at school—they had hair so long they kept it tied back in ponytails. The old man wanted him to have a crew cut, as if there was something wrong about a good head of hair on a man, as if that had anything to do with anything. It wasn't haircuts the old man cared about, it was being able to give orders. With Johnny gone and Liza gone, there was only Bullet to give orders to. You'd think the old man would learn.

Bullet swung his feet back and forth, the weight of wet sneakers pulling at his thigh muscles. The farm lay behind him, all the flat acres of it, broad fields, patches of woods where raccoons and rabbits and squirrels lived, fields left fallow, fields where cornstalks dried in the September sun, lines of loblollies—he didn't look back, he didn't have to, to see it. He looked across the water at the horizon, to the invisible western shore.

The farm was his now, both a draft deferment and a job. If he wanted it. After a couple of years, when Johnny just didn't ever come back, the old man said that to him. "It'll be yours." Ignoring Liza. Bullet just shook his head. The old man thought Bullet was scared of the hard work, but he wasn't, and the old man only thought that because it was an idea he got hold of. The old man got hold of ideas and kept them, clenched tight in his fist, as if that made them true. It was boxes Bullet was afraid of, the kind of boxes the old man built around people he lived with. The draft was a kind of box, too, except that Bullet wasn't so sure he'd mind the army, and he knew for certain he'd make a good soldier; the same way he knew for certain what it would cost him to stay on the farm, waiting for the old man to die.

It wasn't as if his father even wanted Bullet to have the farm. He didn't, he didn't want to let go of the farm ever. Funny, because it was really his wife's farm, her land anyway, the old Hackett place. When they'd gotten married, the old man took over from his father-in-law, who wanted to retire in Florida. The only other person with a claim on it was his wife's sister, who had married and disappeared up north to live with her rich husband. So the farm was his wife's, half of it by law and all of it by rights. But the old man never admitted that, he slapped his name on her, slapped his name on the land, and owned everything. Only, the way he acted and talked, the farm owned him and he hated it. What a life.

For her too, Bullet guessed, living with the old man this way. Except, to watch her work over her vegetable garden, or climb down into Johnny's boat and get the tiller in her hand, he knew she liked it. Whatever the old man did, there was something about her, something proud and bold and brave and strong—the old man couldn't break her, couldn't drive her off. Not if he lived to be a hundred.

The sky grew dark, gray colored with purple, and a few dim stars appeared. The wind blew around him. It was just like the old man to tell him to get his hair cut without giving him a buck for the barber. Do it my way and pay for it with your money. Money Bullet had earned for himself, working for Patrice. Work he'd gotten for himself by going down to the docks early, hanging around, asking if anyone needed an extra hand for the day, doing day work until he met up with Patrice and had a steady job. Hauling crabs all summer. Hauling oysters on winter weekends. Sure, he had the money, he had six hundred and fourteen dollars saved up, and by the end of this fall he'd have enough money to buy himself the sixteen-gauge Smith and Wesson he'd had his eye on for two years. He'd held that gun just once, the only time he'd seen it, at the store in Salisbury. The stock fit into his shoulder like one of his own bones, the triggers moved like a hot knife through cold butter, the balance of the thing made his own twenty-two feel like a Tinker-toy, like the junk it was. He knew what he was saving his money for and it wasn't for haircuts.

With a gun like that, and some practice, he'd—he could see the deer, pronged antlers held up, see it poise for just those crucial seconds listening, see its legs crumple in mid-stride, see it fall while the echoes of that one clean shot still echoed through the trees.

Bullet shook his head to clear the image out of it. He'd learned not to make dreams up for himself, that was part of growing up. Growing up meant you knew what you wanted and you worked for it, and you didn't let yourself get in your own way. Not dreams, not memories—he knew he could allow no weakness in himself if he was going to win free. He could feel the danger of his father's will closing in around him, and he could feel his own strength too. It would cost him, but what didn't cost something? Nothing, that was what. It would cost him this farm that ran acres wide under his feet, that ran acres deep and fertile underneath him. It had already cost him whatever it cost to be different. Nobody knew him anymore—which was funny because all he had done was let his real self out. But everybody saw only the difference. Nobody knew what Bullet was like. Except Patrice. And maybe nobody ever had except Patrice, who didn't mind him as he was, who didn't try to make him into somebody else. Or his mother—she could read him still, he knew, and he could read her too for that matter. But they never talked about that, not in any way. Because it didn't make any difference.

CHAPTER 2

The waves slapped up against the dock and Johnny's boat. More stars appeared. The wind was strong enough to blow the mosquitoes away, so he could stay outside as long as he felt like it. His parents went to bed early. He'd be damned if he'd get his hair cut. He lay back, down on his back on the hard wooden dock, looking up at the star-studded sky, and eased up on himself. It was okay, he was alone.

Maybe he'd grow his hair really long, long as Liza's, and wear it in a braid, or two braids. Bullet grinned—that would give the old man something to chew over.

He didn't blame Liza for just going off with Frank—four years ago now. He almost had to respect her for doing it. About the only smart thing she'd done in her life. Or Johnny either, packing and going off to college and just never coming back; he didn't much blame him anymore. Trust Johnny to do the smart thing, get a scholarship. Johnny got the brains and Liza got the looks.

It was funny though, and not as if he missed her, but he could always feel how Liza wasn't there. Once Johnny was surely gone, it stopped bothering him, like a board nailed into place. But Liza . . . sometimes, like now, when he was alone with nothing to get done and the sky filled up with stars, he could almost hear her, the way she sang. Bullet couldn't sing a note on tune, but he could hear songs inside his head, just the way they sounded.

Now he heard Liza's voice: "Will there be any stars, any stars in my crown," that voice sang, "when at evening the sun goeth down? When I stand with the blest in God's mansions of rest, will there be any stars in my crown?" Well, he didn't know about that, Liza, running off with Frank Verricker like that. He almost hoped they were having a merry old time of it, wherever they were. He liked Frank okay, Frank never let anything get through to him, especially not the old man's hostility. Frank just kept on coming back whenever his ship got into Baltimore. You never knew when he'd turn up, in some rattletrap he'd bought. You never knew when you'd see him slouching against the door-frame, about to bust out laughing. "Tell Liza I've come courting. You're welcome this time too, kid, it's a movie. A couple of hamburgers. Get you out from under, if you want to." Bullet never wanted to, not badly enough to give in to the wanting; and that puzzled Frank, he could tell. The light eyes would study him, curious about what made Bullet tick. After a while, Bullet said no just to keep Frank puzzled. Liza never kept Frank puzzled, she had her heart out there in her eyes for him. She'd hang around waiting for him to show up, out of the blue, whenever. She was surprised every time when she finally figured out that he'd gone off again, back to whatever ship he was on, without a word to her. You'd think she'd have learned, but Liza never did learn much. Or she learned so slow she was long gone before Bullet would have known about it.

Maybe he'd get his hair trimmed a bare quarter of an inch. Then, when his father said, the way he inevitably would, "I instructed you to have your hair cut," Bullet would give him a receipt, or the clippings in an envelope. Billy-O, the barber, would give him a receipt. He'd shove the receipt at the old man, and then what could he say?

Although, when it came to a showdown, the old man wouldn't

say anything; he'd make Bullet's mother do the saying. To pay her back for standing behind Johnny, maybe. She wanted Johnny to go to college; she stood up for that the way she hadn't stood up for anything before or since, against the old man. And Johnny just walked away, never a letter, never a phone call, all that long year. That long year—who knew what she was thinking?—she never said. The old man never said. One long, quiet year that was, not even an explosion when Bullet flunked fifth grade and had to repeat it. All year long, nobody said a thing. That was one good thing about Johnny's leaving. Another good thing was having him gone, with his orders and his right answers, "Cool it, kid," "Hands off." Johnny was always building something, like that boat—working off his temper on wood. Or the tree house for Liza. Talking at Bullet when he caught him messing with his precious tools, because Bullet was supposed to wait until he was old enough to learn how to use them. "Face facts, kid," Johnny told him. Well, Johnny knew how to face facts, and he taught Bullet how, and Bullet had to be grateful for that. "Face facts, you're a breaker. You better learn the truth about yourself." "So what," Bullet answered him, "sew buttons." But Johnny would stand up to the old man, when he wanted, like about Liza keeping OD, and sometimes Johnny could argue him down. After Johnny left, Bullet figured out that he'd also done some standing between his father and Bullet—but Johnny taught Bullet how to stand up for himself before he walked out.

Bullet guessed he didn't fault Johnny, and he didn't fault Liza either. His eyes roamed around, watching the stars. He guessed his mother didn't either, although he knew that she, at least, missed them. Not that she said so, not that she tried to stop Liza from going—but he could read her. And, if he remembered, he remembered how different things used to be, how different she was . . . He could remember seeing her run, her skirt tangling at her legs and himself running to try to catch her and her laughter when she pretended he had—but that was all gone, long gone, faded away, closed off. As far as he could tell, his mother didn't miss it.

Maybe he'd grow braids and wind them up around his head and see how many synonyms his father could think of for effeminate.

Bullet rolled over, sat up, stood up, stretched. Tired. He went back down the dock to the grass. OD was waiting for him on shore. She never would go out onto the dock. Johnny said it was because she had been traumatized by nearly drowning, then explained to Bullet what trauma was. Once, when Liza wasn't around, one long summer day—the first summer Johnny was gone—Bullet had hoisted OD up under his arm and taken her out onto the dock. The water wasn't even deep where he dropped her in, just halfway out the dock. He'd leaned over and dropped her straight down, while her legs scrabbled for a grip on his arms and chest. She didn't howl or anything, just froze stiff and looked at him. Bullet figured, trauma or no, all animals could swim, it was an instinct. But not OD. She sank like a stone, right to the bottom, and he could just barely see her open eyes looking up at him through six inches of murky water. She didn't even move her legs, just like a stone statue. He gave her a while, but she never surfaced. So he jumped in and grabbed her. The scratches he'd had—she was out of her mind with fear he guessed. When he dumped her on the beach she just lay there, shivering. He watched for a while. Johnny was always right about things, Johnny always knew the answers. It was just that the way he told you made you want to prove he was wrong.

"Isn't that right, OD?" Bullet asked the dog. She wagged her tail and hesitated, wondering if she should come closer. He ignored her.

Maybe he'd have it cut in a Mohican cut. He'd seen pictures of those. They shaved away all the hair except for a broad band down the center of your head. It looked pretty terrible. Maybe he'd do that.

If it hadn't been so muggy, he'd have jogged back up to the house, for the pleasure of the run. But he walked, unrelaxing himself: tomorrow he'd get up at five to take the tractor out and get started on the front cornfield, which would give him a couple of hours at the job before the school bus came.

The wind rustled the grasses and night gathered around him. There were a lot of things the old man didn't do anymore, even though he wasn't that old, just sixty. He didn't even put in tobacco anymore. The front fields used to be tobacco—hard work, but a cash crop. Now it was corn and tomatoes, easier to grow, easier to harvest. His father wouldn't think about planting anything else, not even soybeans—which made no sense. Except it was new, of course. Bullet could have done the groundwork and legwork on a new crop, but you couldn't work with the old man, you had to work for him. Bullet wasn't having any of that.

The dirt under his feet was packed hard. Night flowed over him. OD sometimes followed behind—he could hear her—or she'd tear off into the grass to flush out something—a muskrat maybe, a possum, something she never caught. You'd think she'd learn.

Bullet didn't know where the idea came from, like a star shooting in a white arc across the sky. But it stopped him in his tracks.

He threw back his head and laughed out loud. Boy, oh boy. He moved quickly up the path, laughing in pure pleasure.

He would have his head shaved. Absolutely bald. Boy, oh boy.

That would be worth the money.

He ran up the back steps and across the screened porch into the kitchen. His mother was still there, still wearing the white blouse she'd put on for dinner and the blue high-heeled shoes. She looked at him, and he couldn't read her face. She wore her dark hair in a thick braid down her back, the coolest way to wear long hair.

"You've been swimming alone, that's not too smart," she said.

Bullet shrugged. He wondered if she was going to ask him not to, because he wasn't about to not go swimming if he wanted to.

She shrugged back at him. "Are you going to have your hair cut?" she asked. Her eyes didn't give him any messages, one way or the other.

"What do you think?" he asked.

"I'll hear a yes or a no from you," she told him.

"Yes," he said.

"I'll say good night then." She got up from her chair, slow but not relaxed. She never relaxed.

Bullet jammed his hands down into the pockets of his shorts. Then he said to her straight back, "Good night, Maw." He heard the teasing in his own voice. There had been some big fights about calling her Maw, which the old man said was common as dirt, as well as illiterate and ill-enunciated.

She hesitated, then turned around to stare at him.

"You," she said.

He knew what she meant; she used to say that to him, "You, boy," when he was about to go too far. Then she'd either get after him or burst out laughing, and he never knew which to expect. He wondered if she knew what he was going to ask Billy-O to do, then realized that she couldn't. She just knew he was going to do something. She knew it the same way he knew that she knew. He could read her and she could read him—which was the closest they came to talking. *You might say it wasn't too awful close,* Bullet thought, and grinned.

CHAPTER 3

Bullet leaned his shoulder against the cinder block wall of the broad corridor leading down to the cafeteria and watched. They moved on past him like a human river, like a herd of cattle heading for the feed troughs.

If you knew how to look you could see the order within the mass. They moved in groups. Jocks announced themselves by their heavy white letter sweaters with the big red W sewn onto the back—even in this heat. He saw Ted Bayson, the football player, with his latest girl. This one was one of the eggheads, he noticed. Eggheads were marked out by their long hair, boys and girls, and the way their girls didn't hang onto them. They were always talking, mostly arguing. Negroes—blacks they wanted to be called now, "Black is beautiful" was the slogan. *Black is black and that's about all there is to say about it,* Bullet thought. They stuck together, heads like a field of black puffballs with afro haircuts, guys and girls, laughing, touching one another with arms around or with punches and slappings, calling out and heehawing. Even the wimps had their own look, rabbitty around the eyes.

When the corridor had emptied, Bullet drifted into the cafeteria. He liked the way the room was divided almost exactly in half between tables of Negroes and tables of whites. They could pass laws and more laws about integration, they could close down the Negro schools and take "White Only" signs off doors, but it didn't change things. Bullet ran his eyes over the tables, looking for an empty seat. He didn't care where he sat or who he sat with. He sat anywhere he wanted to. Nobody invited him, he was never unwelcome, and that was about exactly the way he wanted things. That day, he slid into the bench beside Jackson and Tommy, across from Cheryl and Lou. They looked up to greet him but went on with their conversation. Bullet pulled his sandwiches out of the paper bag. Tommy he'd known forever. Tommy was a senior now, editor of the paper, with his shoulder-length curly red hair held off his face by a bandana worn like an Indian headband, but Bullet remembered him as a plump boy, back in grade school. They'd been in the same grade until Bullet flunked back a year. Tommy had gotten tiresomely liberal during high school; they were all tiresomely liberal these days, gathering up causes like little kids picking up shells and stones at the beach, all excited and thinking how new and wonderful it was. Waiting to find the stone that was magic, Bullet suspected, the one that would make them brilliant, get their names printed in history books. But they never read the history books and figured out what happened to a lot of people just like them: nothing, at best, and getting wiped out, at worst. Tommy was still okay, he did some thinking. Jackson, Tommy's sidekick for a couple of years now, as well as one of the assistant editors on the paper, was a tall, lean, lazy kid. Bored most of the time and looking for something to stir up; boring all of the time, Bullet thought. Jackson didn't much care for Bullet but didn't have the nerve to do anything about it. The girls—Lou and Cheryl—weren't exactly their girls, weren't exactly not their girls. Lou had a crush on Bullet that she didn't bother to conceal. She was soft, soft wavy hair held back with barrettes, big soft blue eyes. He didn't mind her, much. Cheryl, he respected, for all that most of the time she was around he had the impulse to punch her out. She was the loudest of them, and her opinions came right from whatever magazine she'd last read, and she wasn't too good to look at with her squared figure and little piggly eyes, but nobody scared her, nobody could shut her up. Much as he often wanted to put her mouth out of commission, little as he enjoyed her company, she wasn't as much of a jerk as most other people.

"I actually like a tough teacher," Jackson was maintaining, lying through his teeth. Tommy caught Bullet's eye and looked uncomfortable. "As long as he knows what he's talking about."

"Or her," Cheryl inserted.

"Burn those bras, baby," Jackson said.

"My bra for your draft card," she told him.

"Lay off," Tommy told them. "Don't you ever get tired? I don't know why you bother, Jackson; you've had McIntyre, you know he can't be accused of knowing what he's talking about, so this student teacher might be an improvement."

"McIntyre's mind got lost in 1927," Jackson said. "He's a prime example of a burned-out teacher. If he ever was aflame. Which I doubt seriously. How old is this student teacher, and how did he ever get stuck down here?"

"Do you have him, Bullet?" Tommy asked.

"Bullet wouldn't know, he sleeps through class," Cheryl reported.

"You don't," Lou asked him. "Do you?" She looked as if that was something deliciously wicked.

Bullet took a big bite of his sandwich and chewed it, staring right back at her but not saying anything, until she blushed and looked away. He had looked at the student teacher about once; he was a weedy-looking long-hair with pale skin and a little blond beard about ten hairs thick hanging down from his receding chin. "I don't expect any joy of him," he told them. "But he can't be worse than McIntyre."

"Don't you just wish," Cheryl said.

"Come off it, Cher," Tommy told her. "McIntyre hands out ten dittos a day and then reads them aloud. Aloud. And then you spend the three minutes left at the end of class filling in the blanks he tells you the right answers for, and you hand them in. They're the same dittos he's used for decades. Forty-five minutes a day of screaming boredom. That's what hell must be like," he concluded.

"'Hell is other people,'" Cheryl told him. "Sartre," she informed anyone who might not know, which was, Bullet figured, all of them, including him. Quotes for every occasion, that's what Cheryl had.

"At least McIntyre is always good for a B," Jackson reminded her. "He doesn't know how to give any other grade, his little fingers can't form any other letters. That looks all right on your record."

"Some of us are accustomed to A's," Cheryl said.

"They should fire him," Lou said. "I don't want to have to take the US History course from him if he's not going to teach us anything."

"He's got tenure," Tommy told her. "They'd have to get him on something, to be able to fire him—if they even want to fire him, if they even know how bad he is. Of course, if we could persuade Cheryl here to seduce him . . ."

"Oh wow, can I watch?" Jackson cried.

"Not on your life, you pervert," Cheryl said. "Besides, I'm saving myself for Ted Bayson, the body beautiful. I don't know if Lou would be willing . . ."

"Cheryl," Lou protested softly.

But Cheryl's attention had moved on. "I wonder about Meredith—she's a friend of yours, isn't she, Lou? What is she thinking of?"

"Obviously," Tommy assured her, "she's given up thinking."

"Who's Meredith?" Bullet asked.

They all rounded on him, enjoying themselves. "This year's Bayson girl," Jackson told him. "Don't you pay attention to anything, Bullet?" Tommy asked.

"Nope," Bullet answered. Tommy chuckled, approving and admiring. Even Tommy, who could have figured it out if he'd done any thinking about it, couldn't figure out what had happened to Bullet, to make him so distant. Bullet knew what had happened—he'd grown up. They talked about being grown up and realistic, but they didn't have the first idea about what was really involved in it, so they saw Bullet as some kind of mystery man.

"I never had a student teacher," Lou said.

"Do you think he's dodging the draft?" Tommy asked Bullet.

"He's pretty young," Cheryl answered. "He's about the right age."

"What's his name?" Tommy asked.

"You should have heard McIntyre's introduction of him," Cheryl went on. "'Boys and girls,'" she imitated the wheezy voice, "'we will be privileged this semester to see all the newest methods in education.' I ask you, how can anybody be such a jerk?"

"He probably practices at home," Jackson suggested. "He probably worked for hours on that introduction, making sure it was perfectly jerky. In front of the mirror. What do you think?"

"Oh, I hope not," Cheryl answered. "No wonder he's in a perpetual depression."

"That's stupor," Tommy corrected her, "as in drunken."

"Walker," Bullet said. They looked at him, surprised. "His name's Walker, the student teacher's."

"Besides, if he's dodging the draft, he's got my support," Jackson said.

"My guess is he flunked the physical—have you seen him? He looks sickly," Cheryl told them. "He's probably 4-F."

"Nobody's 4-F anymore," Tommy told her. "They're only using one classification, the typewriters in Washington are jammed and they just keep turning out 1-A's."

"I'll be in Canada before they get a chance at me," Jackson said.

"They don't want you in Canada, swelling the rosters on dole," Cheryl told him.

"If I were a boy—" Lou began, but Tommy interrupted her.

"I'll tell you what it's like," he said. He leaned forward a little, the way he always had when he had an idea that he was excited about. "I've been thinking about this for an editorial. It's like dredging for crabs, the draft. They hang the dredge down off the back of the war machine, right? And they sink it into the mud. Steel teeth grind closed." He demonstrated with his hands. They paid close attention, Bullet saw. "And we're all caught in it, just like the crabs. Scrabbling around in the steel-toothed cage. Dump it out onboard and watch the cannon fodder scrabble around. Get them into baskets and get those lids on tight. That's just what it is. Ship us out in bushel baskets, ship us back in coffins—what's the difference? We can't do any more about it than the crabs can."

He waited for a minute, looking from face to face. "What do you think?" he asked, his eyes coming to rest on Bullet's face.

Bullet shrugged, thinking it was okay, as far as it went, thinking it would make a pretty good editorial.

"They'll never let you print it," Cheryl announced. "You know that. But it's not a bad metaphor."

"I think it's excellent," Lou said. "I think it's a really good metaphor for the draft."

"On the nose, bossman," Jackson added.

They were all, Bullet knew, frightened. Fear sat behind their eyes as they looked at one another. Fear for themselves, fear for one another. They really didn't know, Bullet thought; and maybe you had to grow up in a family like his to know what was really worth being afraid of. They said they argued from moral conviction, labeled it an oppressive war, a dirty war, an imperialistic war, a war for the big corporations—but he knew fear when he smelled it. The way he figured it, you were going to die anyway, so why let fear of that box you in when you couldn't do anything about it.

"Bullet?" Lou's eyes caught his again. He wished she wouldn't do that. "What do you think?"

Bullet shrugged and crumpled up the brown bag with the wax paper he'd wrapped his sandwiches in.

"Bullet doesn't think, you know that," Cheryl announced. "He's a big champion jock. He's our token jock."

Bullet fixed her with a look, and she shut her mouth. "Doing things, or not doing them, because you're afraid," Bullet said. "That strikes me as a mistake."

It took them a minute to figure out what he meant. Then Jackson snapped, "Yeah, but you're the original Fearless Fosdick."

"Bullet does think," Tommy said. "He just doesn't want anyone to find out about it."

"'We have nothing to fear but fear itself,'" Cheryl quoted, her eyes studying Bullet's face.

"Just for once, shut up—or speak for yourself," Jackson said.

"God knows I am scared," Tommy said to Bullet. "But there's a lot more than that involved, and you know it."

Bullet shrugged. He didn't know that.

"Whatever you say." Tommy's voice got sullen.

"Hey, I didn't *say* anything," Bullet pointed out.

"And it's worth being afraid of, anyway," Cheryl said. "It's unrealistic not to be."

"But he wasn't talking about being afraid. He was talking about what you do about being afraid," Lou defended Bullet. He didn't know why she did that—he wasn't looking to win any argument.

"Besides, the draft's unconstitutional," Tommy said. The other three gathered around the argument. Bullet watched them, all leaning toward one another, four heads of long hair, all four of them convinced they could get rid of this problem by talking about it. "Or if not the draft, the war itself. The Constitution lays out the only way that war can be declared."

"You forget that war hasn't been declared," Jackson pointed out.

"Then we're sending in mercenaries. Right? Foreign troops paid to fight somebody else's battles. Besides, the case is that soldiers are fighting. For which our government is paying them. If troops are sent into combat, isn't that war?"

"What're you going to do, sue the army?" Jackson asked.

"Why not? A class action suit—there's a possibility there. At least you could drag it out for years and keep away from the draft."

"Why not just go to law school?" Lou suggested. "The war can't last forever."

"Do you know how long the French were fighting before they pulled out?" Cheryl asked her. "A long time," she answered herself.

"Or the navy," Lou said. "Law school and then the navy."

"I'm willing to consider anything," Tommy said.

"Marriage and procreation," Cheryl suggested. "A couple of babies, fast. Or bigamy?"

"Talk about a fate worse than death," Jackson said.

"I think it's terrible what they're doing to us," Lou said. "To all of us. It really is."

"War is hell," Cheryl said. Bullet watched them react to that.

"What do you know about it?" Jackson demanded. "They don't draft women. They don't even let women into the combat zones, not even near them. You want equality? As far as I'm concerned, you can have it. You can get out there and take your chances with the rest of us. It'll improve the odds for me at least."

"I don't know—the experience might help you grow up," Cheryl snapped.

"I'm worried about living long enough to grow old," Jackson told her. "Growing up will have to take care of itself."

Bullet stood up abruptly. *Jerks.* He'd had enough of their conversation for a day. When they talked like that—and they most often did—it was so stupid he felt like taking a big needle and sewing their lips together. They just didn't know what they were doing, they didn't even know what they wanted to do, if they could do what they wanted. "See you," they said, to his back.

Algebra slid by, and shop. Bullet raised his head from the carburetor he was taking apart, inhaling the odors of oil and sawdust and metal, looking over the long room. Voices mingled with the clinking of metal; the diagrams were drawn out on a movable chalkboard. One of the heads at another table was raised just then, to look at him. The big head nodded, one big hand went up to scratch at the edge of the rolled-up T-shirt in a nervous gesture. Bullet held the eyes but did not respond, and the guy went back to whatever he was doing. This year's test case, and that Bullet could figure out what they were doing didn't make it any less irritating. It had been going on for years. It started the year he stayed back, sixth graders coming after him, seventh graders too. "Rub your nose in the dirt," they'd said, "you dummy." He hadn't minded, and if he hadn't won all of the fights, especially not at first, he'd never been the one to call quits. Two years of it, and it had taken him about that long to figure out what their problem was with him. He wasn't acting the way kids who flunked were supposed to act. After a while, there wasn't anybody who'd come back for a second fight, and then Patrice had asked if he was having the fights he wanted to have or the ones they wanted to have. Things got down to about once a year, then, test cases. That was how he'd met Ted Bayson, who thought he could pound Bullet into going out for football, who wouldn't believe that Bullet just wasn't interested.

This year, it was this vocational track guy from shop. He'd started in right away, the first day of school, pushing at Bullet, looking for a fight. "What do we have here? One of the college preppies come slumming? You come slumming, little boy?" He was big, oxlike, and used to scaring people. Bullet gave him time, gave him nothing to go on. His friends tried to shut him up, but the guy had to show off, wouldn't listen to them. He wasn't too swift. He kept pushing, and when the Negroes on the other side of the big room nudged each other, grinning and murmuring "Go Whitey," he didn't even know they were goading him on. "You with the hair. You and your fag friend, Tommy Hill. Heap big editor. You eggheads make me want to puke."

Bullet just looked at him and waited. *It's up to you,* he thought. *I'm not interested in you. You can dig your own grave if that's what you want.*

"Hey, man, take it easy, that's Tillerman," one of the ox-guy's friends said, pulling back at the thick arm.

"Tiller-man? You gotta be kidding. Looks like Tiller-girl to me. With all that pretty hair." His friends didn't know whether to laugh like they were supposed to, or what.

Bullet waited, letting his anger boil slow: when people were this stupid and wouldn't listen because they didn't listen to anybody . . . and wouldn't leave him alone. . . . It burned him, the way people thought because he was built small they could take him on, or walk all over people just because they were over six foot and heavy; they thought they could run him scared. *Jerks.*

"I'll see you in the parking lot after school, Tiller-girl," the big jerk said. Bullet had shrugged, had met him and had blacked both of his eyes before he let him go bleed on his friends for comfort. He'd figured out before he got there behind the pickups what the guy should get. Two black eyes, to mark him for a week and get the message out clear for this year. A couple of punches to the diaphragm so he'd drop his guard, then wham! The guy had been knocked to his knees by the first real punch Bullet delivered. Bullet had to wait for him to get up before he could black the left eye.

"Hey," the guy had said, surprise making his voice high, starting to back away, "I didn't—"

Bullet got at him again, diaphragm, eye. *I know you didn't and what you didn't. Didn't think I'd show up, did you? Didn't think I'd be able to touch you. And now you want to back out, but it's your fight. You wanted it, now you've got it, and let's finish it.*

When Bullet had finished it he walked away, to wash off the blood on his hand from the guy's nose and get on down to practice. Ever since, the guy had tried to be friendly, sort of nodding and keeping a respectful distance. He even tried apologizing, "Hey, man, I'm sorry, I didn't know—"

"You didn't put up much of a fight," Bullet cut him off, the only time he'd spoken to him. People like that—bullies who stepped on other people just because their feet were big enough—they should be put down. Like runts. They were as bad as the fear-run people they stepped on, who toadied around them. Bullet didn't want to have anything to do with any of them. Every year one of them would try him out, somehow. Every year he'd have to show whoever that he wasn't to be messed around with, then they'd all leave him alone. He didn't know what their problem was with him, although he could guess—some kind of King of the Mountain game. One thing he could say about the Negroes, they never tried him out; they seemed to know he had nothing to do with them.

CHAPTER 4

After school, Bullet jogged down to the field, without changing. He ran in sneakers, and in hot weather he just wore a pair of shorts to school under his jeans. Bullet didn't mind practice. The coach left him pretty much alone. The coach was a big guy, over two hundred pounds, but in good shape for all of his fifty-odd years. He'd played baseball good enough for collegiate championships in his day. He coached baseball in the spring, track in the fall and filled in with gym classes during the winter. Summers he worked as a lifeguard for a pool up in Delaware. He'd always known enough to leave Bullet alone, ever since Bullet showed up in the fall of ninth grade. The track team wasn't much, mostly guys who couldn't make the football team but were too serious about sports to want to take gym. The coach worked them, keeping track of them all, sprinters and milers, high and long jumpers, hurdlers, pole vaulters, javelin throwers and the cross-country too. They each had to enter three events, he told them, because the school had to have four people in each event to hold a meet against another school. Bullet did javelin throw and high jump, with cross-country. Once the coach had asked him to do the fifteen hundred meter run, or hurdles, because he was fast, but Bullet wouldn't. The first year he was on the track team, he'd run the relay, but after that he picked his own events. His run was cross-country, and he didn't want to use up energy on any other running event. He usually came in somewhere between second and fifth in high jump and javelin, depending on the competition. He'd never lost a cross-country race, never even come close to losing. The team was always invited to the state championships, but the school never placed because the rest of the team wasn't good enough. You got ten points for a first, but only five, three, two for the other places. Only Bullet could collect the ten.

He didn't mind, he'd been state champion for two years. The coach minded some, but Bullet couldn't help him with that. If you didn't have the talent to put on the field, you just didn't have it. Bullet's accumulated points over the season got them into the championship trials and that was all he could do for them.

The first part of practice Bullet spent warming up with a few jumps and throws. He took it easy. If he jumped over six-and-a-half he started landing wrong, pulling muscles or bruising joints he needed in good working order for cross-country. He could get up as high as he wanted, higher than any of the other jumpers, but he took it easy against the risk of spraining or breaking something when he came down. "You land like some rag doll, Tillerman," the Coach said. "You've got to roll with it, use your shoulders."

Bullet shrugged. He could get high enough.

A two-mile cross-country trail had been laid out behind the field, so familiar that Bullet could run it without thinking—which wasn't much use to him. That day, early in September, the coach stopped Bullet as he went over to start the runners: "That new guy, see him?" Bullet nodded, his eyes on the tall Negro with heavy, muscular legs, long thighs and short calves, who stood away from the other two cross-country entrants, both white. "He might be okay for cross-country. He's a hurdler, pretty good."

"Okay," Bullet said. He knew what the coach was going to say next, he always knew. *See how he goes,* he predicted.

"See how he goes."

And don't try to run him out this first time.

"And don't try to run him out this first time."

Bullet didn't say anything. He stood in the sunlight, waiting to be given the nod to go. The coach nodded to him.

The Negro approached Bullet, near the start. He held his hand out. Bullet didn't take it to shake. The Negro acted as if nothing had happened. "Name's Tamer, Tamer Shipps. He tells me I should run cross-country."

Bullet didn't say anything. This Tamer looked older than most high school students, he looked about twenty—but Negroes tended to look older; they aged differently too, something to do with the skin, he figured. The old Negroes around town had white-gray hair, but their skin didn't look dried-out and papery. The other two runners were a tenth and eleventh grader. Neither had the musculature of this Tamer, or Bullet either. Tamer had close-cropped black hair and deep brown skin, broad nose and full lips, and, under heavy eyebrows, eyes that looked awake.

"Okay," he said now. "I read you, Whitey. Just tell me what to do."

"Run," Bullet said. "Run as fast as you can and keep running."

"You sho' does make it sound fun, massa," Tamer said. His mouth didn't move, but his eyes looked amused.

Beats picking cotton.

Tamer had a broad, stubborn jaw, and it looked like he needed a shave. They stared at each other for a few seconds. Bullet shrugged. Tamer's big shoulders straightened. They moved apart, going separately and at different rates to the starting point, where a broad dirt path entered a stand of pines. The two other runners came to join Bullet. "Hey," they said without eagerness. "Hey, Bullet." He nodded at them, raised one arm and then let it fall abruptly to start them off.

The two-mile course made a big circle. It covered no hills,

neither were there any ditches, but it crossed some fields and a couple of creeks. It wasn't much of a course. But people were more interested in football, basketball and baseball—that was where the money for fields, coaches and equipment went. And cheerleaders and uniforms. It didn't hurt Bullet any; it just pissed him off to have to run on such a rinkydink course. He ran the practice the same way he ran every race: he took up an immediate lead and pulled farther ahead with every step. He ran alone.

Up rises, leaping shallow gulleys, splashing through the creeks where muddy bottoms caught at his shoes—he ran beside a tomato field with just a few fat globules ripening on the vines now, the bright greeny red of late-season tomatoes. He couldn't hear anything, nobody. His legs stretched out, the pace fast and steady. He picked up his pace a beat after the first half mile, held the new pace for a quarter mile and then, rounding a big cornfield to head back for the mile, picked his pace up again. He breathed steadily through his nose. He never got out of breath. A real runner never did, because it wasn't lungs that took the strain, but muscles. The hardest thing for Bullet about the daily practices was to keep driving his pace. He knew the course so well he didn't even have to think about where to put his feet or how to take an obstacle—even the section through overgrown woods had a path trampled through it, and all you did was scratch your legs as you went through. So Bullet used the practice times for his own purpose: he ran three-quarters of it at top speed and worked during the last quarter to improve that.

Back at the starting point, his legs feeling good, the sweat running over him feeling good, he waited around for the others to come in. The two underclassmen had been running the course for a week and a half now; they should begin to come in at a jog at least. The first couple of times around, he'd had to wait twenty minutes or half an hour for them to come walking and groaning in, trying to pick up their knees to a shambling gait when they saw him watching. By now, they should be able to get some kind of pace over the two-mile course. If they would do any practicing at home, of course, it would be different. But nobody ever did. For the first two or three meets, Bullet could be sure he'd be the only Crisfield runner to finish out a course. Somehow, these guys seemed to think if they could run two miles they could automatically run the three or four of a race. He had no sympathy for them. He kind of liked watching them creep across the finish lines of the meets and bend over to vomit.

But it was the Negro who came first into view, after a long wait. His T-shirt was soaked with sweat, his chest heaved, he jogged steadily. As Bullet watched, he stumbled over a buried stone and fell flat. You had to be pretty tired to let a stumble like that knock you flat. Bullet watched as he brought himself back up to his knees, then up to his feet, then—leaning forward, barely running at all—start jogging again, stubbornly. Light brown dust caked his legs and arms in splotches. His thighs and arms and face shone with a coating of sweat that ran in rivulets through the dust. He breathed through his open mouth, breathed hard. When he came up to Bullet, just over the finish, he fell full length onto his hands, like a reverse push-up. He lowered himself onto the ground and lay there, facedown. His back heaved. His hair was beaded with water. His eyes were closed.

The other two jogged sedately into sight. Bullet looked at them. They hadn't changed their pace for the last stretch, and they talked as they jogged. He looked down at the Negro. Then he turned and went to take a shower.

Negroes did well in the marathon; it seemed like it was always some guy from Ethiopia or Africa who won it. So it wasn't surprising that this Tamer had come in ahead. It didn't worry Bullet, it barely interested him—it showed up how worthless those other two were. *Somebody should go behind them with a bullwhip,* he thought; *get their asses going.* Bullet grinned to himself. He could do it; he could make them, but he wasn't interested. He wanted a shower, then he was going downtown to see Billy-O. Nobody ever ran cross-country more than one season, nobody except Bullet. It was just too hard.

Bullet slid into his chair at the center of a long side of the wooden table. At one end his father sat—a platter of fried ham slices in front of him, a bowl of rice, and a plate of corn-on-the-cob beside him—wearing a tie and jacket. Three plates were stacked up in front of him. A bowl of sliced tomatoes was in front of Bullet. Bullet had a glass of milk. His parents had water. His father's hands were under the table, folded in his lap; the eyes were fixed on the hands. Bullet's mother sat straight and still at the other end. As soon as he heard Bullet's chair scrape into place, the old man started reciting grace, the same every evening: "For what we are about to receive, the Lord make us truly thankful," he said.

He served the plates, Bullet's mother first, then Bullet, then himself; a slice of fried ham, a spoonful of rice, an ear of corn. "There's no reason to eat in an uncivilized manner just because we're poor," his father had said so often Bullet used to believe that was what he meant, that was why he required them all to dress for each dinner. But he'd figured out, finally, what the old man was really up to, that it was just another order he was giving. Bullet passed his mother's plate down to her and caught her speculative glance. He pulled the knitted watchcap down further over his ears and waited.

It wasn't until everybody had been served that Bullet's father looked at him. "Pass the butter," he said and then, his eyes having slid over Bullet, "Take off that hat."

Bullet obeyed. He reached up and removed the woollen hat,

dropping it onto the floor beside his chair. His mother looked up at him, then quickly away. Her dark hazel eyes flashed briefly, Bullet saw, and her mouth twitched, before she settled her face into expressionlessness. She picked up her knife and made a quick cut into the slab of meat.

Bullet waited for what his father would say and ate his dinner while he waited, ate slowly and methodically.

"I'll take some mustard," his father said.

"There's none," his mother answered.

After a while his father said, "We'll need more butter."

"We're almost out," his mother answered. "It's time to do a shopping."

"I won't be going into town for another week. Or more."

Bullet's mother looked down the table, then nodded, her mouth still. She'd have to sail in, then, two to four hours, depending on how the wind lay; and if a wind was whipping up waves or it rained, the bags would get wet and disintegrate carrying them up from the dock. Too bad.

"I'll need some money," was all she said.

"I can spare fifteen dollars," his father answered. Bullet reached out to take two more ears of corn—at fifteen dollars for a week's food, they'd be eating hungry. His father wouldn't touch crabs and never had, wouldn't have the smell of them in the kitchen. Too bad, because crabs were free for the trapping. Any fish she could get cheap downtown could only be eaten the same day, with the long sail to spoil it; chicken, too, was likely to turn in this hot weather, with the long midday calms when sails flapped uselessly and the tide carried you where it was going.

"I said cut"—the old man spoke to him now—"not shaved."

Bullet shrugged. *And what are you going to do about it?*

"There's long precedent for adolescent rebelliousness." His father spoke to his plate. The man had pale eyes and white hair in a crew cut. He was a big, spare man, like Johnny. "Aristotle refers to it. You won't know who he is."

Oh yeah?

"Just because there's precedent doesn't mean I find it tolerable."

Tough on you.

"I don't want to lay eyes on you until it's grown out."

Bullet shrugged. *Then keep 'em closed, old man.* Billy-O had told him it needed shaving every day or so.

"He won't be eating with us now."

Bullet's mother nodded. Her hair was getting long streaks of gray in it, woven down through the braid.

"You needn't bother fixing anything for him, he can see to himself. You'll eat with me."

She nodded again, not saying anything.

"Since he's determined to have his own way, he can have his way all to himself."

Fair enough. He could run before he ate now.

Without looking at him, his father asked: "Do you hear, Samuel?"

"Yes, sir," Bullet answered. *And if you think I care, you can think again.*

"Then why are you still sitting here?"

CHAPTER 5

Bullet watched the trotline rise up out of the dark water. The thick pieces of eel with which it was baited had white underbellies, so that up until nearly the surface, in the dim light, it looked like there was a crab on every piece. This was the first run and most of the bait came up empty. He kept his net poised just above the surface of the water; he kept his eyes on the moving line. Behind him, Patrice ran the motor, holding the boat on course and on speed. One after the other, the chunks of bait thumped against the plastic roller. The big engine chugged away.

Finally a crab rose, holding onto the eel with one claw while ripping at it with the other. Bullet dipped, netted it, dumped it into the waiting basket. As he had expected, this crab was the vanguard for a cluster—he netted three in a row, one after the other, dropped them into the basket and waited again.

The surface of the water lay still, dull silver. A low, flat wash of clouds covered the rising sun. The motor hummed.

They were alone on the bay. No other professionals worked Sundays, and the amateurs seemed to think that Labor Day marked the end for crabs as well as people. This was the way Bullet liked it best. They set the line out across the mouth of a creek and had everything the way they wanted it. As they progressed along the line's length, crabs appeared in bunches. Bullet got them on board, into the basket. When they came to the end of the line, Patrice flicked the line free from the roller, turned the big boat in a broad circle, and headed back for another run.

After the second run, Patrice shut down the motor. They had almost a full bushel—not a bad showing, not a particularly good one. Most of the crabs in the basket had settled down, but the newest ones still moved restlessly, snapping their pincers at each other, establishing their territory on the pile of crabs. Their beady eyes barely showed up against the grimy blue of their shells. Some had foamy spittle coming out of their mouths, blown out in impersonal hostility. They waved their claws up in the air, threatening. Bullet put the lid on top of the basket. A couple of swimmer claws stuck out between the vertical slats.

"We will have started too early, I think," Patrice said.

Bullet leaned back against the gunwales and nodded at his employer. Patrice had short, tightly curled hair, graying irregularly. He wore, as always, khaki trousers, heavy workboots, and no shirt. His face and torso were tanned a permanent deep brown; even his potbelly, swelling out over his belt, shone brown. He was a couple of inches shorter than Bullet, and barrel-chested, with big muscles in his shoulders and arms. He had about the ugliest face Bullet had ever seen, little dark eyes and a short nose, big flat teeth and skin marked with deep lines.

"Well, so we have erred," Patrice said cheerfully. Nothing bothered him. In the more than four years Bullet had been working for him, he'd never seen Patrice bothered, not by people, not by weather, not by bad luck or good luck. "That makes it a good time to eat. I'll put on the water for the coffee." Before he went up to the little three-sided cabin near the bow of the long workboat, he leaned over the side to call up the opaque water of the creek: "Crabs, awake! Arise! Breakfast is now being served! Good, salted eel marinated in a rich brine! Come to the table, crabs!"

Bullet had baited that line: it took ten solid minutes of washing, first with salt and then with lemon, to get the smell off his hands. "They're not that stupid," he said.

Patrice turned to look at him, squinting into the glare of the sun, which was emerging from the cloud cover. "You think not? See now, I give you an analogy. You are sitting at your dinner table. You are eating—perhaps fried chicken, perhaps a beef stew with biscuits. You notice that your plate rises from the table. Slowly, it rises up, up, through an open window, toward the top of the sky. Do you then hold tightly to your plate, so that you attend it, yourself rising to the sky? Do you then continue to eat, as you and your plate soar up, up, higher and still higher? No, I will tell you, you do not. You say to yourself, 'Bullet, old friend, something is not right.' You let go of the plate. And do you know why you act so? Because you are smart."

"Nope," Bullet said, shaking his head, grinning. "It's because I'm not a crab. Because my instinct for self-preservation is stronger than my instinct to feed."

Patrice studied him sadly. "I don't know why I waste myself on you. You have no speculative thought. I don't know why I hire you."

"I do," Bullet answered. "Because I work."

Patrice went up to the cabin. Bullet rested against the gunwales, with the boat rocking gently under his feet as it drifted with the tide out toward the red road the sun made on the silver water. The temperature rose. It had taken him a while to figure out Patrice. In fact, the first time Patrice had offered him a permanent job he had refused. Skippers who hired kids did it because they could give them much less of the take, and Bullet was then just thirteen. He didn't mind working for Patrice, even then, but he'd learned how things were: Skippers thought they could bully kids around more, because kids were so glad of any job. Kids got all the scut work, too.

Not Bullet, though, he'd never go out more than once with a skipper who kept him busy cleaning up, more than his fair share. He didn't mind being yelled at, up to a point, or blamed because the wind was up and the crabs weren't biting, or the engine broke down. Up to a point. He'd learned, too, just how much talking back he could do, just how far he could go. He kind of enjoyed that, pushing a man just to the exact point and then, when the guy was dying to have you go one step farther so he could really explode at you, stop. He always paced himself, too, in the work; how fast he'd move. These guys, all the guys on the crew, whoever they were, they thought because they were bigger, older, stronger, in command, they could tell him everything and use him as a yelling board when something else went wrong on them.

Patrice had made no sense to Bullet at first. He never got riled, and Bullet couldn't push him at all. He'd shrug things off. When he felt like talking, he'd talk; Bullet could listen or not, depending. When he talked, it wasn't the usual stuff, women or hard luck or boasting. He didn't ask questions either, he'd just start in, about someplace he'd been, or something he liked to eat, or even some old story he'd thought of. Bullet figured, at first, that the guy was a little weird and he steered clear. But after a while, he figured it out: Patrice had nothing to prove, nothing to prove on Bullet, nothing to prove to him. He let Bullet be. So the second time, the summer between seventh and eighth grade, that Patrice asked him to work regularly, Bullet agreed. If nothing else, Patrice always did a fair split of the take, so Bullet could give him a fair day's work without getting cheated, whether he was a kid or not. Patrice worked him like a man, paid him like a man, treated him like a man. From the first.

When Patrice came back, he carried a metal tray on which were a tin coffeepot, two thick white mugs, a slab of butter, and a straw basket covered with a white cloth. Patrice ground his coffee beans the last thing before they left the dock, because the fresher the grind the better the coffee. The crusty rolls under the cloth had been in the oven when Bullet arrived at five that morning. The missing fingers on Patrice's hand, which made it difficult for him to tie bait onto the line and tiring for him to net crabs, didn't impede him in the kitchen.

They sat down facing one another, cross-legged on the wooden deck. Bullet's stomach felt hollow with a hunger he hadn't felt until just then. He broke a roll apart with his hands and spread it with butter. Patrice poured coffee.

Patrice was missing the thumb on his right hand and the first two joints on the index finger on his left hand. He'd never told Bullet how that happened, but Bullet assumed from the thick, calloused stumps that it must have been long ago, and Patrice no longer remembered that he had lost anything. He never mentioned it, never had.

"Good," Patrice said, swigging coffee.

"Good," Bullet agreed, his mouth full of chewy white bread, the mug ready to hand.

Patrice looked at him, his little eyes bright and clever. "Now that your scalp is tanned you don't look so appalling."

"Did I look appalling?" Bullet hadn't thought about it.

"You didn't think so? You looked like . . . you were wearing a helmet, a leprous helmet. You looked savage, a barbarian." The eyes studied him. "You still do."

"I like it," Bullet said. He didn't think about what he was going to say to Patrice, he just said what he felt like.

"How do you keep the growth down?"

"Shave it every other day."

"Troublesome, isn't it?"

"Yeah, but it's worth it."

"To annoy your father?" Patrice guessed.

Bullet smiled. "Besides, what's wrong with being a barbarian?"

"Of course, there's something splended about that. And you do have a good head, my friend, well-shaped. But when you consider the centuries that have gone into the civilizing of the world . . ."

"Yeah, but has that worked?" Bullet asked. He drained the last of his coffee.

"No, perhaps not. Ah, well." Patrice poured him another half cup and refilled his own. "But you are young, and there is hope for you yet."

Bullet didn't answer. Patrice often teased him this way and there wasn't anything he needed to say in answer. It was just the way Patrice got around to talking about something he wanted to talk about.

"You know, traditionally, the barbarian has swept over the civilized world," Patrice said now. "Goths—or Visigoths—or Ostrogoths—and the Vandals, and the Huns. Poor old Rome, like a kitchen floor, swept and swept, don't you think? The Achaians at Troy. The Vikings along the coasts of Ireland and England and France."

"Are there any barbarians left?" Bullet wondered.

Patrice shrugged. "Can a man tell about the history he lives in? The enemy is always the barbarian, just as God is always on my side. The blacks in Africa, perhaps they are."

"Come off it."

"Tall, strong and splendid—warrior races? You are thinking too narrowly, you must look out for that. Picture him, his dark skin gleaming, bare feet, and his body hung with jewelry made out of the bones of his prey, he moves through the long grass. A spear held high, only a skin shield to protect him. He stands before an elephant. If he kills the beast, he is a hero. If he dies—

all a man asks is to die well, to die in good battle and bravely; he is a hero."

"You're prettying it up," Bullet said.

"But of course, this is speculative thought."

"You ought to come to school and see what they're really like."

"If I did, I might not agree with you about what they're really like. And there's you—you're a barbarian—out of your time. But you will have trouble, being only one. It is hard for one to overrun."

Bullet guessed he knew what Patrice meant, and he didn't mind it. He'd always known how different he was, and he'd never minded.

"You're pleased," Patrice observed. "I have paid you a compliment?" The gnome face looked as if it wanted to laugh.

"You have," Bullet told him. "You know, you don't *talk* like you're uneducated."

"But why should I. I have been to school. I was even going to go on, in school."

"What happened?"

Patrice shrugged. "The Germans came."

"And?"

"I no longer went to school. Finish your coffee and get on with your work. I'll save the last roll for you."

Bullet did as he was told, he never minded doing what Patrice told him. He'd learned that Patrice only told him what was necessary. Bullet stood up to get the tongs. He lifted the lid of the basket and looked down at the quiet mass of crabs. He tonged one out and turned it over, to see by the apron whether it was male or female. They sold females to the packing houses, the different sizes all jumbled in together. It was the jimmies, the males over six inches from point to point, that they were really after, but as long as a crab was of the legal size they could use it. This one was a male, barely five inches, and he tossed it into the basket for the small males.

Behind him he heard Patrice move to stand in the small shaded rectangle made by the cabin. He knew how his employer would look, leaning against the cabin wall, a mug in his hand, his eyes watching Bullet cull the catch. He'd always let Bullet do the culling and never griped at any mistakes. A couple of times, at first, Bullet had tossed big jimmies overboard, watching them arc out over the water, listening for any sound from behind him that Patrice had seen the loss. Finally, getting no reaction, he had flipped one that must have been seven and a half inches, maybe even eight, really big. He'd waited, to see what the explosion would be like. But he'd heard only a chuckle, and then Patrice had spoken behind him. "I cannot bear to watch, you are on your own." Bullet had turned around, angry at the laughter in the man's voice; but Patrice was already walking away, to lift the cover up and take a look at the engine.

Sometimes Bullet wondered why Patrice had put up with him at first, but he never asked. He just kept coming to work, feeling himself ease up as soon as he stepped over the picket fence into Patrice's yard. He didn't mind Patrice, and Patrice didn't mind him; they did all right together.

Bullet worked fast, tonging, turning, tossing either into a basket or overboard. The crabs were stirred up now, moving around over one another, spitting, clacking their claws. As he held each up, it swam with its legs in unresponsive air. He tonged in and sorted, ignoring the most aggressive ones for a while. These backed away from the tongs, pincers upraised, legs scurrying for footholds on the wet and moving mass beneath. He gave them time to settle down while he picked out another. Once they had settled down, folding their claws in together, he picked one out quickly. They would take the jimmies down to the dock to sell by the bushel at whatever the day's price was. Buyers from the small crab houses all over the eastern shore came to the docks at about lunchtime; Patrice preferred to sell to them because he got a better price. At this time of year, however, he would probably have to sell to the wholesalers, and they would make less.

Bullet bent to dip into the basket, straightened to toss the crab overboard, bent again to dip again. There was a rhythm to this job, governed by the movement of his arm, like scything through a field of hay. Behind him, Patrice stood watching, watching Bullet do the job right. Until the culling was done, they couldn't tell what the harvest of the catch actually was.

"Looks like a couple dozen," Bullet reported. "Not too terrific." He corroborated the expression on Patrice's face.

Patrice handed him the roll, slathered with butter. Bullet bit into it, hungry again. "It is early days. We'll see how the runs go. Maybe it's time to start for oysters."

"It's pretty warm still."

"You prefer when we oyster in the winter?" Patrice raised his eyebrows.

Bullet knew he was teasing. "Frankly, I prefer crabbing. Oystering is hard work."

"It's all hard work. You're young and strong. I'm old and wily. Hard work doesn't hurt us."

"I didn't say it did," Bullet pointed out.

"No, you didn't," Patrice agreed. "Ready now?"

CHAPTER 6

After all, it was a fair catch for the seven hours of work: three bushels of big jimmies and five for the canning firms, which they sold at the town dock just after noon. Bullet's share came to fifty dollars, a quarter of the take. It was after one by the time they had berthed *Fraternité* at the dock in front of Patrice's house, hosed her down, checked gas and oil in the engine, rebaited the trotline, and coiled it into the plastic garbage can at the stern. Once, Bullet had asked Patrice why he had named his boat *Fraternité*. Most of the workboats had women's names, *Loralee*, *Helen*, *Polly*, *Zena*. Patrice had just smiled like some old gnome who had lived a hundred years and shrugged. "And you spelled it wrong," Bullet pointed out. Patrice laughed and explained about the old motto. "*Liberté* and *egalité*," he said, teasing, "they are the ideal. But *Fraternité* is humanly possible. I make my statement," he said.

It was weird, but Bullet didn't mind. Patrice played with ideas, speculative thought, he called it. He was always thinking about something, and he liked it when Bullet listened, but he didn't try to make him pay attention. Patrice didn't even care about being right. He didn't, Bullet thought, following his employer down the long dock, care about much of anything. About thinking, and he liked to eat, he cared about food, and he liked Bullet, liked having him around. Patrice was free, which meant he made his own rules and followed them. Bullet admired him.

Besides, Patrice didn't think like anybody else, he always had some odd angle. Once, a few years ago—it was right after Liza left, that was when it was—Bullet had been working away, doing something, and brought down a stack of baskets so hard half of them were smashed. He felt better, for a few minutes, less burned up. Then he wondered if Patrice had seen and turned around to catch the anxious eyes looking at him. *Go ahead, fire me, you'll never get anyone who can work as hard as I can,* Bullet had thought, bracing himself. But Patrice wasn't angry. He wasn't frightened either, or threatened. "You are so angry, my friend," he had said.

"So what?" Bullet demanded.

"What makes you so angry?"

"None of your business," Bullet had said.

"Granted. But when someone like you is angry, I am interested in what causes it."

"I'm angry most of the time," Bullet told Patrice.

"Yes? Why?"

"People, the way they act. Things, the way they are."

Patrice nodded his head once, on an ah-sound, and turned back to the motor.

"I'll fix the baskets," Bullet told him.

"Do you know how?"

"No, but I can figure it out."

"I'll show you. Later. Now we have work to do."

"You're a real slave driver, Patrice," Bullet had said.

His employer laughed out loud. "Me? I think not. I can't be. If I am, you're the worst slave in the history of man's injustice to man."

Bullet had grinned, and turned to picking up the splintered mess he had made. And he had fixed the baskets too. Patrice had shown him how, then had left him to do it.

While Patrice made lunch, Bullet took a long, hot shower.

They didn't have a shower at home, only a big old tub with claw feet. When he emerged from the bathroom attached to the back of the one-room house, he wandered around the little yard while Patrice washed up.

Patrice had no grass, no garden, and only one little pine growing in the clayey soil. A low picket fence surrounded the plot of land that he rented, its white paint bright and clean. The yard was crammed with outboards and dinghys, each at some different stage of repair. Patrice bought or salvaged these boats and motors, fixed them up and sold them at a profit. That day, he had three boats, the longest fourteen feet, lying upside down in a row, on top of logs. Several motors, from three to twenty horsepower, lay around. Some of them had the casing off and the parts spread out—spark plugs, pull cords, propeller blades. It looked messy but was, Bullet knew, kept neatly, as neatly as the cabinets inside where Patrice stored his paint and tools and spare parts.

They ate inside, at the card table. Patrice had made a thick potato soup, which he served with sandwiches made out of the rolls, split and stuffed with meat he had chopped and mixed together with boiled eggs, olives, and green peppers. They ate without speaking, until they were full. Patrice poured himself fresh coffee. Bullet refilled his glass from the tap. Patrice lit a thin cigar.

"All the same, we will be oystering soon. I should take down the tongs this week."

Bullet looked up to where Patrice kept his oyster tongs, hung on the wall. Their twelve-foot handles and thick, stubby rakes looked as heavy as he knew they were. The metal of the teeth glowed with the careful cleaning Patrice and he had given them at the end of last winter's season. "Okay," he said.

"Such enthusiasm," Patrice said.

Bullet changed the subject. "You got a new boat."

"I found her washed up into the marshes. She looked salvageable."

Bullet snorted: "It looks to me like you'll be replacing more than half the thing."

"So? Did you also notice she is not so broad as most fourteen-footers? She would have been a fast little boat."

Bullet just shook his head. Patrice always salvaged and rebuilt. He threw nothing away. He worked with metal and wood, soldering, sawing, refitting. "What else is there for a man to do in the evenings?" he asked. He didn't expect an answer.

Evenings, Bullet's father read books, silent at his desk, alone in the living room with the door closed. His mother baked, preserved, knitted, sewed, cleaned. Bullet stayed away: Most evenings of the year he ran; in winter he withdrew upstairs right after dinner, up to the second floor he now had entirely to himself. The other two bedrooms were empty except for furniture; the first thing his mother did, after Johnny left, after Liza left, was take their stuff up to the attic. Winter evenings, when it was too cold to run, Bullet went up to his room and did nothing. He could have done homework during the winter, but he never did it at any other time and couldn't think of any reason to make an exception for winter.

Johnny, he remembered, would be in the kitchen, building something or looking at library books with plans, or doing his homework, or reading. Liza might help their mother, or sing at the piano if the old man wasn't around; sometimes she would play checkers with Bullet. She always lost. Even at Parcheesi she always lost. And Johnny always won—well, he was years older, bigger, smarter, faster. He could always make Bullet do what he told him. He wouldn't mind taking Johnny on now, Bullet thought, *I could hold my own and maybe then some.*

He bit into another of Patrice's sandwiches, almost wishing Johnny was still around, to show. But that was all before, anyway, before Johnny started locking horns with the old man. As Johnny got older, it was like that, like two bulls in one yard. Dinners, year after year, night piled up on night, and the old man always got the last word. Except about college, and then it was their mother who tipped the scales.

"There's nothing you can't learn here," their father kept telling Johnny, "while you learn how to work the farm that'll keep you in food."

"You just don't know," Johnny had answered. "You don't even know how much you don't know, even about farming."

The old man chewed on that one for a while, while everybody sat quiet. "Children always think they know better. They never do. You'll be staying here, and if you've got the character, you'll study," he finally said.

"You haven't got any say in it, not anymore," Johnny told him. "I've got a scholarship, I don't need anything from you."

"I don't see you putting your own food on your own plate," the old man said.

"You know what I mean," Johnny muttered.

"I know how unrealistic you are," the old man said.

"I'm going," Johnny said, stubborn.

"College is a luxury, and we can't afford luxuries," the old man told him.

"I'm going," Johnny said.

Finally, Bullet's mother broke in. "Then go, and let's have this question settled. Unless you settle to stay."

Johnny looked at her: "You want me to go, don't you?"

Her mouth moved, but no words came out. Liza's fat tears spilled out of her eyes, but she didn't say anything. Bullet knew his mother didn't want Johnny to go, not the way the two of them were using that word, to mean go away and stay away. "Yes," she finally said, "go."

Bullet opened his mouth to stop Johnny, who was scraping his chair away from the table, but she said, "You, boy, keep your mouth closed."

Johnny looked at her again, at that, but he didn't know what she meant, and he was supposed to be so smart; even Liza knew what she meant, and the old man sat smug and smiling tight at his end of the table. Johnny went, figuring he'd won out after all, and the old man figured he'd won out, and Bullet knew then it didn't do any good to be smart, that being smart didn't keep people from boxing you in. The two of them, they'd boxed her in, and they'd boxed themselves in. But nobody was going to get Bullet that way, he made up his mind to that.

"But, Pop," he remembered Liza starting to say. Bullet kicked her hard, in the shin, and she looked at him then and shut up. Which was what he wanted her to do.

He thought, finishing the sandwich, finishing up his bowl of soup, his belly full now, that if he'd been Liza he'd have kicked him back. But Liza didn't. Maybe she knew how useless it was, anyway. He never could tell what Liza knew, anyway. That night she had just got up to clear the table and help with the dishes—which was what Bullet did now, too. He took the plates and bowls and piled them by the sink. Patrice finished his coffee, then—holding the cigar between his teeth—offered, "Let me show you what I'll do with her." They went back outside to look at the fourteen-footer.

It had once been painted, but the coats had worn down to a dusting of colorlessness over the weathered boards. It looked as gray as a dock. Gaping holes had been smashed through its floorboards.

Patrice put his hand on the curiously rounded keel. "This is called carvel-planking," he told Bullet, his palm following the curved line of wood back to the curved transom. The planks on the sides, except for a couple of places, looked okay, but the gunwales were mashed down, sprung loose as the ribs of the boat had twisted with whatever strain it had been subjected to. The transom was useless, split down its center.

"Even you can't do much with this," Bullet said.

Patrice leaned forward to pull one of the floorboards up. "I will enjoy trying. See how they are grooved to fit? Beautiful. It must have been rough weather to damage something this well made."

"You think maybe it floated up from the ocean?"

"No, the ocean would have broken up even this boat. The ribs are sound, and the sides. I'll replank the bottom. I've never attempted such work—" and Patrice was off, talking about the steps of it, cutting the length to match, cutting the board to square, then planing it down to the right curve to run from stern to bow. Bullet listened with half an ear, he wasn't interested. Patrice just liked talking. He didn't mind that, and Patrice didn't mind if he listened or not. "I'll need to find some oak," Patrice concluded.

"That'll cost you."

Patrice shrugged.

"Planing it yourself will take hours. You'll never make your money back on it, Patrice."

"Oh well, I'll have put real work into it, and that is something too."

"Besides, who has the money for a dinghy like that, anyway?"

"She'll take fifteen horses when I finish with her. Can you see how she'll look? White, clean and white, with maybe a blue stripe showing at the waterline. I'll let you help with the painting."

"You're going to paint oak?"

"Sometimes a man just wants to do the best he is capable of. And why do you yourself run your races, do you ever think of that?"

"What're you going to ask for it?"

"With a motor—the right motor—five hundred dollars. Maybe six."

Bullet shook his head. "We'd better go after some oysters. You're going to need the money."

"And you, my friend, you also. Perhaps I will sell her to you?"

Bullet laughed. "No chance. What would I do with a boat? But you ought to paint it red, if you're going to paint it. Fire engine red."

"You think so? No, I don't agree."

"Anyway, I've got to go. I've had my orders for the weekend."

"Is he punishing you? For the hair?"

"He can't do anything. He just refuses to have to look at me, no big deal."

Patrice studied Bullet briefly, out of thoughtful brown eyes. "Your father puzzles me," he said. "I feel sorry for him."

"I don't."

"No, of course not, and why should you? You're his victim. But I've never met the man, and he has no power over me, so I feel sorry for him. Which matters nothing, not to him, not to you, not to me. Do you have one of your meets next Saturday?"

"Yeah. The first."

"Good luck to you then, which you do not need. I'll look for you on Sunday."

"Oysters?"

"We'll know that later in the week."

Bullet jogged the five miles back to the farm. He plowed the second field along the driveway that afternoon, plowing under the dried and broken cornstalks, burying them into the earth to rot and fertilize. As he pulled the tractor out into the driveway, he looked back at the lumpy brown field ready to hibernate for the winter, as if he had pulled a blanket up over it and tucked it in. Fed it too, he thought to himself, turning the tractor into the empty barn. He shoved the sagging barn doors closed behind him and went into the kitchen. They were eating, some kind of hash made out of ham and potatoes. Neither of them looked at him as he ran a glass of water then stood at the sink to drink it.

"We need engine oil," he said, speaking to the center of the table.

Nobody said anything for a while, they just ate away. Bullet turned to put his glass down.

"You might start a shopping list, Abigail," his father's voice said. "I may be going to town at the end of the week."

Bullet felt his hand tighten around the glass—he could break it, and easily, crushing it, letting the splinters pierce his hand. He put the glass down carefully and looked out the window over the sink, toward the vegetable garden and the marsh grasses beyond. What the old man was doing was forcing her to sail into town for the groceries. The old man didn't like messing with bags of groceries. Or something. There wasn't anything much left to eat, not even canned soup. Bullet was going to have oatmeal without milk for the third night in a row. Oatmeal they had in abundance. And she'd do it too, because she never just told the old man there wasn't anything to eat, or gave him oatmeal.

"Those barn doors need rehanging," his father's voice said behind him. It was an order.

You don't think I can, do you, on my own. Hanging doors, especially doors that big, and with the hinges rusting up and the wood behind the hinges rotten—that was at least a two-man job. They'd been getting worse and worse for a couple of years. Now they dug into the ground when you shoved them closed. If he hadn't been so pissed, Bullet could have laughed at how obvious the old man was.

Bullet walked out of the kitchen, moving slowly down the path to the dock, to run. Halfway there, OD emerged from the golden grasses, wagging her tail to greet him. "Get away, you stupid mutt," he told her. She stood wagging her tail and watching him as he passed her by.

CHAPTER 7

Bullet waited in the broad doorway of the lunchroom, paper bag in his hand, looking things over. Lou caught his eye, then indicated with a tilt of her head the empty seat next to her. He slid his eyes past her, not even glancing at the other three. That Monday he went to sit with some of the football squad.

Bullet slid onto the end of the wooden bench, and the four others on that side slid down to make room for him. "Hey man." "How they hanging?" "Long time no see." "Hey, Bullet, have a meatball," offered Jim, who pronged one from his green plastic plate of spaghetti and leaned across the table to shove it at Bullet's face. "It's not really shit, it just looks like it. And tastes like it. You want some?"

"You're kidding." Bullet unwrapped his packet of sandwiches. Just jam this lunch; they were out of peanut butter. It was lucky his mother bought flour by the hundred-pound sack and saw to it that the old man always picked one up when he went into town. They never ran out of bread.

"Where you been?" Pete asked.

Bullet fixed him with his eye: "In school." They laughed.

"Okay, okay, I never laid claim to brains," Pete said. He twirled spaghetti around his fork and ate a mouthful, sucking in the strands that hung out. He held his fork like a hammer in his huge fist. "How're you guys going to do in the meet Saturday?"

"I'll win," Bullet told him.

"We *know* that," Jim said. "That doesn't interest me. I might be interested if you lost one. But how about the rest of you. Anyone any good?"

Bullet shook his head, chewing.

"You should play football," they told him, once again. "We win sometimes."

"Bullet doesn't play team sports," Pete told them.

"That's the ticket," Bullet agreed.

"Why should you, if you're a potential Olympic contender?" Jim needled.

Bullet shrugged. "I'm not contending."

"Your coach thinks you are."

"That's his problem," Bullet said. "What about you, when's your first game?"

They groaned. "Man, we already played it. Saturday. Don't you read your school paper? *The Crimson Blade*?"

"Bullet doesn't read, doesn't write—he's a tribute to the school system."

"How'd he get to eleventh grade?"

"He just ripples his muscles at the teachers. Women faint. Men get terrorized. He used to run his fingers through his hair—" They laughed.

Their laughter was swept away in a silence that brushed over the entire cafeteria, from one end to the other. Bullet finally turned around to see what had attracted so much attention.

A big Negro stood at the cash register, his eyes scanning the room. As he moved toward the tables of Negroes, low conversations started up again.

"That guy—," Jim muttered.

"If there's one thing I can't tolerate," Pete agreed, "it's an uppity nigger. He thought"—Pete grinned at Bullet—"he'd play football."

"He's big enough," Bullet said.

"Maybe," Jim agreed. "But he's not quite white enough. We had a little talk with him. Have they integrated you guys?"

"Yeah."

They digested this fact.

"Don't you care?"

"It's got nothing to do with me."

"Just because nobody keeps up with you personally," Jim argued, "you've still got to think about the principle of the thing. Whose side are you on, anyway?"

Bullet just looked at him.

"On his own, Dumbo," Pete answered for Bullet.

Bullet didn't much care to have anyone answer for him.

"You know, man, sometimes," Jim told Bullet, "that's not good enough. Times like these. Where's he come from, anyway, this guy? Anybody know? He's not one of ours, ours know better. This nigger is trouble, capital T, trouble. You can smell it on him," he told the listening table. "What's his name? Tamer? The names they give their kids, it's a joke. But you watch, he'll turn out to be some organizer from up North. Five'll get you ten he'll be walking into the student lounge one day. Black as the ace of spades and cool as a cucumber."

"Let him try it," they growled. "Can't be too soon for me."

Bullet crumpled up the wax paper and brown bag.

"Has anybody seen that trig test yet?" Pete asked.

"It's not a test, it's a quiz."

"Anything that takes a whole period is a test. I need to get the answers. If I don't pass that course with a C the University won't look twice at me. On account of me not being an Olympic contender."

"So what?"

"So I'd rather not be drafted next summer."

"Oh, I dunno," Jim said. "It'd get you out of Crisfield. You know, see the world. Kill off a few of the little yellow guys."

"Even I know how dumb that is," Pete answered.

"Why freak yourself out about it, it's not even October yet."

"We got bigger problems right here. Bigger, browner ones."

"Yeah, well, I still want to see that test. Quiz. Whatever you wanna call it. Pass the word around, okay?"

"What is it, you scared of the army? You chicken?" Jim asked.

"You looking to get your face messed up? Then I wouldn't say that, buddy. I wouldn't even think it, if I was you."

Bullet rose, tossed his garbage into the overflowing trash can and moved away. "See you," they called after him.

He drifted through the corridors, not even wondering anymore about their inability to face up to facts, just because, when they were together they made themselves feel that they were okay, because they all didn't face facts together. He went past the student lounge, a big room down by the principal's office. It had been a classroom until two years ago, when a bunch of seniors had gotten up a petition to have a student center. Nothing happened until the parents got into it, and then things happened fast. The principal always folded under parent pressure. He gave the students the room. They filled it with any furniture they could find—old sofas, chairs, tables nobody else could use and ashtrays. The place was a mess, always smoky, papers all over the floor and chairs, people sitting around. Bullet looked in the open door and walked past, through a cloud of cigarette smoke and loud voices. By unspoken agreement it was whites only.

He went on down the hall and up two flights of stairs to algebra. All around him, locker doors clanged shut. Bullet never took anything to class: they could make him show up; they could make him sit there; but they couldn't make him carry things around with him. If he needed paper or pencil, the teacher could supply it. If he needed a book, he'd look over someone's shoulder—or do without. He didn't care. The teachers pretty much ignored him once they figured it out. He passed the courses and that was all that mattered to them, getting the kids through the courses and out.

As that week went on, Bullet became aware of some mounting tension, in the halls, in the lunchroom, even in classes. It was like the tension in a bus going to a meet where you didn't know how you'd do, some team you'd never run against before. Muttered remarks, too low for a teacher to pin down, got made across a classroom. Everybody was touchy, or too quiet. Everybody looked around a lot, watching everybody else. "A little experiment in escalation," Jackson called it, over lunch on Wednesday, his eyes glittering, looking nervy, looking pleased with himself.

"Bullet's not interested," Cheryl said, warning Jackson to keep his mouth closed.

"I think you underestimate Bullet," Jackson said. "He's smart enough, and he can't be as hard-hearted as he acts. Nobody could be. Is that right, Bullet?"

"You tell me," Bullet answered.

"Okay, I will. We've agreed, at last, that maybe the Civil War is over, and maybe the South will not rise again. Now it's time to bring this place into the twentieth century. So we've been doing a little talking, making an encouraging remark here and there, a discouraging remark there and here."

Bullet asked, "Why?"

"Didn't I tell you?" Cheryl asked.

Jackson groaned. "Because you can't make an omelette without breaking eggs," he told Bullet, angry now.

"It's not an omelette you're making," Bullet pointed out.

"Sounds like you're afraid to rock the boat," Cheryl challenged him.

Bullet didn't bother answering.

"C'mon, Bullet, you know that sometimes things have to blow up before any kind of progress can be made," Tommy said.

Bullet looked around at them. They were too smart to let themselves act like such jerks, but they still did. They thought that just because they were smashing eggs they must be making an omelette. He shrugged: too bad.

"I'd like you on our side," Tommy said to him.

Cheryl saved him the trouble of answering: "He's not on anybody's side, except his own."

Bullet looked up out the high windows, where rain sluiced down, then back at his plate. He was eating a cafeteria lunch. They'd finally run out of everything at home, and he wasn't about to eat plain slices of bread for lunch.

Later, practice was called because of the rain, but Bullet ran the course anyway. There was no law guaranteeing that it wouldn't rain during a meet, and maybe even rain just like this, hard and cold, an autumnal rain, pelting down where the wind blew it. He took a long hot shower in the gym before he went into town.

At Tydings' Grocery, he asked Millie to cut him three steaks. He always fed himself steak for the three nights before a meet. "About ten dollars worth," he told her. At the front of the store, he picked up a jar of peanut butter and a dozen eggs, plus a gallon of milk. These he placed on the counter where Herb Tydings sat looking out at the pouring rain. Herb ran the store. His wife, Millie, was the butcher. Herb had pale soft skin that always looked freshly shaved, and round, rimless glasses. "Looks like the weather's finally going to turn," he remarked. "So I guess it's about winter, wouldn't you say?" Bullet didn't answer. "Your mother was in earlier—like a drowned rat she looked. I told her so. She said she couldn't speak to the rat part, but she knew she wasn't drowned." He chuckled. "She's sharp, Ab is. I could do with seeing more of her."

Bullet looked to the back of the store where Millie slowly weighed in his steaks. It didn't do any good to get impatient with Millie. She never hurried anything, not her big body, not her hands, not her mind. But she could cut a steak to within twenty-five cents of the price you asked her for, every time.

"You know, I never see your father," Herb continued. "I'd think maybe he was dead, except then I'd have read about it in the paper."

Bullet snorted. *Me too,* he almost said.

"Will you be running on Saturday?" Herb asked him.

"Yeah."

"Good luck to you," Herb said. He always knew what was going on, he always talked to the people who came in, asking about their families, the crops or the catch, health, news, something. Herb Tydings kept up with everybody. "Though you don't need luck, do you?"

"Nope," Bullet said.

"You will though, everybody does, sooner or later," Herb advised him. Herb talked, whether his customer wanted conversation or not. "Everybody needs good luck, everybody gets some bad luck. It's not the luck, is it?" He didn't wait for Bullet to answer. "It's how you take the luck you get. I mean, we all of us our age went through the Depression. Talk about bad luck. Your father isn't the only man who got his plans changed by the Depression. Or the war."

"He wasn't in the army."

"Because he had the farm, they didn't draft farmers. Me, I got into the Quartermaster Corps, and that was good luck. Life always surprised you, and I guess some people don't take to surprises. What about you?" he asked.

Bullet didn't answer. It had been a long time since anything had surprised him, good surprise or bad surprise. But Herb didn't expect an answer, he didn't wait to hear one. He reached out to take the wrapped meat from Millie and calculated the price on a pad. "Nine eighty, that okay?"

"Fine." Herb totaled the bill. Bullet paid, thanked Herb, waved to Millie and left. He stood a minute on the covered porch, while the rain pounded down onto the road. He put his grocery bag under the poncho he wore.

It would have taken her a couple of hours to sail back, Bullet knew—she should have let the old man go hungry for a day. They had bread, and he didn't know why she didn't just wait for the weather to clear, or the old man to give in and drive her. After a dinner of plain bread he'd have found something urgent to do in town, Bullet would put money on that. They both of them made him angry.

He splashed through puddles, going out of the town center and down to Tommy's house, next to the long cinderblock building where Mr. Leeds had his seafood plant. Tommy was alone at home, working on layout in the dining room. He had spread articles and pictures all over the table and he looked glad to take some time off from the job, to drive Bullet home. "They vetoed my editorial with the crab metaphor," Tommy told him, as soon as Bullet pulled the car door closed behind him. "I dunno, Bullet, I'm thinking of resigning in protest. We can't talk about Vietnam, or the draft, can't even hint at integration. I didn't sign up to work on a mouthpiece for the establishment; that isn't how I want to spend my time. What would you do?"

"Quit," Bullet said.

"Agreed," Tommy said, then sighed. They drove slowly, the wipers flipping back and forth across the windshield. "But you always did have the guts to do what you wanted. I wish I was like you."

Bullet didn't bother answering that. He knew as well as Tommy did that that wasn't the truth. Tommy enjoyed being Tommy Leeds, editor of *The Crimson Blade;* he'd fought a hard campaign to be elected to the position and he took pride in the paper he brought out, he took pride in the editorial work he did.

"But if I quit they'll have won, don't you see?"

"No, I don't see that. It's not a matter of whether they win, but of whether you lose," Bullet pointed out.

Tommy smiled at that. "If I thought you cared enough to tell lies, I'd accuse you of logic chopping," he said. "But since you don't—"

"I don't," Bullet assured him.

"Unless I could maybe start up an underground newspaper. A real student newspaper. What do you think? Would you like to have a real student newspaper?"

Bullet didn't say anything.

Tommy laughed. "Okay, it was a dumb question, I know you don't read. I wish you were a senior, man, I'd like to sit in some classes with you. You're a good influence. No, I'm serious. But how you stay smart beats me. You're weird, Bullet, an absolute weirdo. Even before you shaved your head to look the part. You're absolutely unconnected. Why else do you think I listen to you?"

"You don't listen to me," Bullet pointed out.

"Well, more than I listen to anyone else. I'll be damned if I'll quit the paper."

"I know."

"They can't make me."

"That's right."

"We do get some stuff in, we get some past them. They'd like me to quit, I think. I may be flattering myself, but I think they would."

"If I were them, I would."

"Yeah. So I won't. Besides, what's the point of life if you don't do something about it, about all the things. Seriously, Bullet."

The car had pulled up by Bullet's mailbox, where Tommy always let Bullet off. Bullet waited a minute before getting out, to answer Tommy. "Are you sure there is any point?" he asked.

Tommy started to answer quickly, then stopped himself. Bullet opened the door.

"That's the question, isn't it? The real question," Tommy said. "You're something, Bullet, you know that? A loner. You'd better get running. I'll see you."

Bullet jogged down the rutted dirt driveway, splashing through puddles. His poncho kept the bag of groceries dry, but the rain beat down on his scalp. That was one bad thing about not having any hair—in a cold rain it really got to you, right away. Too bad, Bullet thought.

He was too late to get his dinner cooked and eaten before his parents had theirs, so he put his groceries away and went upstairs. His mother was in the kitchen, with a chicken in the oven; he could smell it, so he guessed she'd made it in from town all right. "I'm back," he said, before going on up to his room. The farm used to have chickens, and a couple of cows too, when she was a child. There were stalls in the barn, empty for years and years now, and a wooden butter churn in her pantry under the shelves where she kept the tomatoes and beans she put up all summer long. Now there was only OD and a tractor and the pickup.

Bullet opened the door of his wardrobe—a big square piece of furniture, with cowboys and Indians Liza had painted on it, why he never knew—and lifted out the twenty-two he kept wrapped in an old towel on the floor of it. He unrolled the towel, then took some oil to the stock. He'd figured he could get something as trade-in for the twenty-two, when he went up to Salisbury for the Smith and Wesson, so he kept it looking good.

When he heard the kitchen empty, he went downstairs. He put the steak on to fry, and while it was cooking he took a flashlight out into the vegetable garden. His feet squelched down into the muddy soil and the rain soaked his shoulders. He was hoping to find a couple of late tomatoes, but all he could see that was ripe was a zucchini, so he leaned down and broke that from its thick stem.

He was sitting at the table, eating slices of raw zucchini, the thick steak and some bread and butter, when his father came to the door. Bullet knew the man was there but he didn't look up.

"Have you forgotten about the barn doors?"

"No," Bullet said.

There was a long silence. Bullet cut himself a big bite of steak and chewed. He spread butter around another piece of bread.

"I asked you a question."

I answered it.

"Don't think you can avoid the job. You still have your keep to earn."

Bullet felt his hand tighten around the fork, but he ate as methodically as before. After a while he heard the footsteps going back down to the living room where his father had his desk and his precious books. He heard the door close. He heard his mother on the back porch starting to run wet laundry through the hand ringer of the old washing machine she still used, because until it broke down there was no need to get another. So his mother thought the rain would stop in the night. Usually, his mother was pretty good on weather. Saturday's meet was up beyond Easton, where the land was a little hillier and two days of rain would leave the course muddy, underneath a deceptive dry layer. Usually, the land could absorb one day's rain.

CHAPTER 8

A westerly wind was blowing the sky clear as Bullet slid into his desk. The bell rang. First period, US History, and they hadn't seen even McIntyre's nose since the second week of school. Rumor had it McIntyre was spending the semester between the faculty lounge and the local bar, while Walker taught his classes.

Walker usually gave them a minute or two to settle down while he checked off the roll; then they got to work, taking quizzes, reviewing the reading, discussing. Bullet stretched his legs out. Funny—nobody was having any trouble settling down that morning.

Walker stood behind the big desk at the front of the classroom. He looked around. He seemed to be listening, standing there at the front, his eyes roaming. He looked young, permanently underfed, and had that wimpy beard—but he was doing okay. He seemed to know what he was talking about and he kept shifting tactics on them, so he was always running things. He didn't give Bullet any trouble, either, no trouble at all. Bullet didn't mind him.

"I see," Walker said. "It looks like we'd better do some thinking about it."

Bullet didn't know what he was talking about. The rest of the class did: there was a restless movement, leaning forward at their desks, and a babble of voices rose on questions and arguments.

"What are they going to do about it?"

"Who's responsible?"

"I think it's terrible, just terrible."

"Serves him right, if you ask me."

At the tail end of the outburst a girl's voice wailed, "I don't understand, I don't understand it at all, I don't understand what's happening," and another outburst began.

"Everybody knows how things go here, he asked for it."

"But what's going to happen now?"

"Hold on," Walker called. "Hey, wait a minute. Hold on," waving his hands up in the air until he had their attention. "I said think about it. I haven't heard any thinking."

"What's to think about? We all know what happened and we all know why." That was Cheryl from the front row, sounding impatient and sure of herself.

"You know, Miss Haskins, one of the most rewarding things about history is that it teaches us how much we don't know. The case of Richard the Third is a good example—do you know about Richard the Third?" Nobody did. Nobody wanted to. "Then I'll tell you, but not today. Mr. Tillerman—do you know what happened?"

Bullet shook his head; he wasn't about to be dragged into anything.

"But you can't use him for an example of anything. Bullet never knows, he doesn't care, he doesn't pay attention to anything," Cheryl argued.

"Bullet?" Walker asked her. He looked at Bullet, but not as if he had asked a question. Bullet just stared back at him. "He seems to know enough to pass the course," Walker said. "So you can't say he never, can you? There's a lesson in that. So suppose we start with just what did happen. Facts."

"Four whites jumped a black guy—"

"There were eight of them the way I heard it and—"

"I heard five—"

"Outside the parking lot—"

"That's not on school property—"

"And beat him up."

"They were all kids. Students. Here."

"Nobody knows who they are."

"Yeah, but we can guess."

"They split before the cops got—"

"Except the black—"

"He couldn't move, the way I heard it."

"His name's Tamer, Tamer Shipps," one of the black students interrupted. Until then they'd all sat quiet. "And they were wearing masks I hear. Your guys. He hadn't done anything."

"He went into the student lounge."

"He's a student, isn't he?"

"Yeah, but . . ."

"But what?" Walker asked, into the uncomfortable silence.

"But everybody knows they don't go in there."

"They?" Walker asked.

"Blacks. He knew, everybody knew he was going to try something."

"There's no law—"

"There's a law that says he can. In fact."

"Yeah, but everybody knows how we live with that—"

Cheryl's loud voice cut across the argument. "Let's forget that. There is a law and that is a fact. Like there's a draft law. It's a law that forces people to do what somebody thinks they ought to do. What's important to me is, I'm not in favor of four to one odds in a fight—"

"Five."

"Eight."

"Whatever the number," Cheryl overrode them. "What we're missing here is motive. Why. Why this Tamer went in there. He knew, didn't he?" she insisted across the room at the blacks.

"We all know," they answered.

"Then why did he try going in there?" she demanded.

There was a long silence. Walker outwaited it.

"Because," Cheryl finally continued, "if you go looking for trouble and you find it, you have nothing to complain about."

"He is not complaining."

"It's you who's complaining, far as I can tell."

"He wasn't looking for trouble. He was looking for a place to sit down out of the rain."

"And you forgot to ask why your guys had to beat him up, while you're asking why. We all *know* why there were four of them."

There was another silence. Bullet watched the class, watched Walker watching.

A white boy changed the subject. "What I want to know is what they're going to do about it. I mean, I figure I know why this Tamer went in there and I think he's right—well, I do—but I want to know what they're going to do about roughing somebody up."

"What do you think should be done?"

"It wasn't on school property."

"Let it blow over, it won't happen again."

"You believe that?"

"You know who they are, your guys—I bet. You've got to know. They broke the law, assault and battery. They should get thrown out of school. We would be and you know it."

This time Walker took over the silence. "This isn't thinking you're doing. Start to finish, you're not thinking. You're judging—do you know what I mean?" They didn't. "Motive may call for judgment, but the law is beyond that."

A babble of protests arose.

"Laws just guarantee the status quo, the position of the people in power."

"You're confusing law with justice, Mr. Walker."

"You believe in the *law*?"

"Laws can be wrong, everybody knows that."

He waved his hands again to silence them, and after a while they piped down, unsatisfied. He turned around and started writing on the board:

These, in the day when heaven was falling,
The hour when earth's foundations fled,

"That's poetry, this isn't English class."

"Shut *up*, you jerk."

Followed their mercenary calling

"Mercenary, that means money, I'm for that."

"What does this have to do with anything?"

And took their wages and are dead.

"What kind of a poem is that, Mr. Walker?"

"At least it's not all about beauty and love."

"It's not even a poem, all it does is rhyme. It doesn't have the right language."

"What about heaven falling, that's a metaphor or whatever, isn't it? Heaven doesn't fall."

"Unless you're Chicken Little." They laughed.

Walker ignored them and wrote on:

Their shoulders held the sky suspended,
They stood, and earth's foundations stay;

"Aha! Parallel structure."

"I get all I can take of this in English."

"Why doesn't he say anything? What's the point?"

What God abandoned, these defended,

"Now we know who the bad guys are."

"Unless God is the bad guy."

"How much longer is there till the period ends, anybody got a watch on?"

And saved the sum of things for pay.

"I get it so far, let's see what the third stanza says."

"What do you mean you get it, the thing doesn't make any sense at all."

"It's not supposed to make sense, it's poetry."

"Think Walker's gone off the deep end?"

There was a third stanza. Walker wrote underneath the last words: EPITAPH ON AN ARMY OF MERCENARIES—Housman. Then he turned around.

"Well?" he asked.

They all kept their eyes on the board, not looking at Walker. *Wow,* Bullet thought unwillingly. He caught Walker's pale eyes on him and wiped his face clean of expression.

Finally someone said, "You don't write the title at the end, it goes at the top."

For a minute Walker looked blank, and Bullet hoped he'd blow up. But he didn't. "What side is Housman on?" he asked. "You know what mercenaries are?"

"Yeah, us in Vietnam."

"How does Housman feel about mercenaries?" Walker asked.

They argued it back and forth, with Walker stepping in only when he had to say, “We’re not interested in how you feel about mercenaries, but with how Housman feels.” Bullet didn’t listen to the argument, which had nothing to do with him. He kept his eyes on the words chalked onto the board. *An epitaph is what goes on a tombstone,* he thought, *cut in with a chisel, and boy is that right for this.*

Shortly before the bell rang, Walker made his point: “This poem is thinking, as opposed to judging.

“Use it as a model, okay?” Walker asked the class. Then, “Can anyone guess what Housman did for a living?”

“Soldier.”

“Something physical, athlete?”

“Poet.”

“Nobody earns a living as a poet, jerk.”

“I think he was a mortician. I mean, it’s very depressing.”

“Big game hunter?”

“Doctor?”

“Lawyer?”

“Indian Chief?”

Walker shook his head solemnly. “Mr. Tillerman?” he asked.

Bullet stared at him. *What do you want with me?*

“Can you narrow it down? Do you think he was educated?”

“Sure,” Bullet said.

“Why?” Walker insisted.

“Teachers always do that, use educated men as examples,” Bullet answered. It wasn’t what Walker wanted him to say. He knew what Walker wanted him to say, about the way you had to have worked on your mind to be able to do that, like you had to work on your muscles to bring your stride down exactly right.

Walker seemed unoffended. But he told the class, briefly, that Housman was a college professor who taught classics, in England,

and then that they could leave the room. "But it's five minutes," they told him. He dismissed them anyway, "Except Mr. Tillerman. Could I have a word with you?"

Bullet stayed in his seat. Walker came over close to him. *Now what.*

"You liked it, didn't you." Walker indicated the board behind him. Bullet shrugged. "I want to talk to you," Walker said, "because I don't seem to be able to . . . make any connection with you. The other students don't seem to . . . like you. Although they don't dislike you. In fact, they respect you."

None of this made any difference to Bullet. But you had to look out for guys like Walker, they kept looking for ways to get inside you. And they weren't dumb. He kept his face deadpan, his eyes fixed on Walker's little pale eyes. Walker stood there.

"How did you get a name like Bullet?" Walker asked.

I named myself, which is none of your business.

A pale, foolish smile moved Walker's mouth. "Have it your way, but if there's anything you want to talk to me about—well, I just want you to know I'm here, if you need to talk."

Bullet stood up, impatient with this. He didn't have to stay and listen.

"Because you don't strike me as happy," Walker said, "and—"

"I've got a class to get to," Bullet interrupted. He left the room before Walker could see that he was about to burst out laughing. The guy was a jerk, a smart jerk, but still—not smart, educated. Him and his beard and trying to get people to think: a few years of teaching would show him what was what.

The cafeteria that day was quiet, but it hummed with the intensity of subdued conversations. Bullet sat down with the wimps, who shifted over to give him lots of room. They didn't know what to say, after hello, and they were smart enough to keep quiet, keep their eyes down. Bullet ate, and looked around. The usual, he thought: tables of whites, tables of Negroes—the wimps occupying the no-man's-land in between. Bullet noted missing faces among the whites. He scanned the tables to see if the big figure of Tamer Shipp was there. He thought he'd recognize the guy. He couldn't be sure, but he didn't think Tamer was in the room. That made sense, if he couldn't even move out of the cops' way, but he wondered about the whites—there were a few possibles among the absentees. Lying low, probably.

Bullet chewed, taking in the tension that filled the whole big room, just like the light from overhead fluorescent bulbs filled it, getting into every corner, flowing under the tables and showing the way feet were planted on the floor, ready to run, tense. Guys ate hunched over their trays, their eyes not on the people they were eating with, but scanning the room. Girls kept their eyes down, not looking at anyone, not talking much.

"Gee," said one of the wimps, a scrawny tenth grader with thick glasses and a madras shirt, "I'm staying home for a few days."

"How can you get away with that?"

"My mom'll get my dad to let me, when I tell her. I'm not coming back *here* until this cools down."

Chicken.

"When things—blow up—it's people like us who really get trampled. If I were you I'd have an asthma attack."

They looked like they were having heart attacks right then, pale and rabbitty. Bullet just ate his sandwiches, biting, chewing, swallowing. Part of the tension in the room was fear. You could taste it—dank and metallic—colored fear and white fear. Bullet slowly emptied the two pints of milk he'd gotten, slowly got up, slowly left the room.

* * *

The next day the lunchroom jingled with heightened tension as Bullet moved unremarked to the wimps' table. Only a couple of ninth grade girls there, he noticed, and a half-dozen little eighth graders. He was early, to watch the room fill up, the long line by the service counter moving along smoothly, the people carrying their trays over to tables. Voices rang louder than usual. Ted Bayson had a gap in his mouth where a couple of teeth used to be and was chewing cautiously; there were a couple of limping guys, a couple of black eyes. They'd gotten a little trouble, then.

A big colored guy stood, looking around the noisy room—that was Tamer, Bullet recognized him, he'd remember him now. The guy had really heavy eyebrows. His face looked swollen and he was moving as if it hurt, but his glance all over the room was cool enough. The room was quiet, too quiet. Then it got noisy, but too noisy. Bullet shifted his feet under the table: as if school wasn't bad enough the way it ordinarily was; he didn't need to spend his days in a war zone. But everybody was ready to panic. The whole room was ready to blow up around him.

Tamer moved down the center of the room, heading for the back where some friends waved to him. He was nodding his head in greeting and going between two tables, when he tripped and fell. The plate and silverware and metal tray rang on the cement floor. The milk carton fell under him and squooshed milk out, over his shirt. The room was so silent you could hear the bowl that held Jell-O ringing round and round and round until finally it rang around belly up and was quiet.

Bullet watched, his hands relaxed on the table. Nobody spoke. The silence rang around the room. Most people hunched over their lunches like nothing had happened and nobody had noticed, except nobody was eating anything.

Tamer got up slowly. His face had a gray-green undertone. Ketchup from the hamburgers was on his shirt front, mixed with milk. Jell-O hung off his cheek.

Laughter—low, muffled—started on Bullet's side of the room. Bullet didn't move his eyes to see who it was.

"D'jew see that?"

"Who got him?"

Bullet shifted his legs out from under the confining table.

For a minute, nobody moved. But there was a kind of growling noise, somewhere.

Then a bunch of blacks flashed into action, and from a nearby table whites stood up to match them. Wooden benches scraped back on the floor. Voices cursed, called. People headed for the door, crowding and pushing. People closed in around the fight, pushing.

Bullet caught a glimpse of silver and moved—the whites were vocational track and he knew how they liked to fight, he knew who their leader would be. He brought the leader down with a tackle that put the guy's wrist under Bullet's hand: he wrapped his fingers around the wrist while his shoulders pinned the guy to the floor; he closed his finger around the wrist until he felt the bones in there rubbing up against one another. The knife fell onto the floor, a black-handled switchblade. Bullet got up and dragged the guy after him, whipping his arm up behind his back and pushing, hard.

"What're you doing?" the guy asked. "Leggo of me."

Bullet didn't answer. Out of the corner of his eye he saw a hand reach down for the blade on the floor. He slammed his foot down on the fingers, then covered the knife with his shoe. He spoke into his man's ear, loud so everyone could hear him. "Not in here." The last thing he wanted to put up with was a riot. That wasn't even clean fighting. There was a way to get your fighting in, if you wanted to. These people just—didn't know anything, he thought to himself in disgust.

"What the—"

Bullet jerked up, sharp up, on the arm.

"You hear me?" he asked. The head nodded. Bullet looked around at the rest of them—just staring at him. He looked across and saw only Tamer's back, where he faced a bunch of coloreds. Dark eyes glared at the boys among whom Bullet stood.

"Sit down," Tamer said. Ordered. Muttering, they obeyed him.

Bullet let his man's arm down and spun him around to look into his sweating face. He didn't say anything, just stared into the guy's eyes until he was sure the message had gotten through, past the anger, and past the fear pain brought. Then he turned and left the room.

"Thanks, man," low voices murmured at his back.

CHAPTER 9

The sun had risen into a clear sky when the coach stopped for Bullet by his mailbox at six forty-five. They drove on down to the town dock, where the school bus waited. Bullet climbed into the yellow bus and took his usual seat, right front, by the window. The rest of the team trickled in, one after the other, waiting until the last minute before climbing onto the bus. The coach checked them in, calling out names and making marks on his clipboard.

They were down to three Negroes, Bullet noticed; one of them Tamer, of course. The Negroes moved on to the back of the bus, where all three could sit together. The meet was at a school three hours north, up in Queen Anne's County. Bullet slouched down in his seat, relaxed.

He could hear nerves in the rest of the team, sitting behind him. He could see nerves in the coach's body, hunched by the opposite window. Bullet wasn't tense. He was going to run, there was nothing to make him tense about that. He didn't remember the course. He never remembered a course from one year to the next. He didn't want to. He wouldn't jog it either, although that was how you prepared for a cross-country run—you were supposed to jog over the course an hour or more before you ran it and plan your approaches and learn the obstacles. Bullet never tried to study a course. That was no way to train your reflexes, or find out how your quick judgments were. That was the way if what you wanted to do was win.

As time passed, the bus behind him alternated between uneasy silences, quick low conversation, and loud nervous joking. Bullet never turned around, didn't measure the distance by passing towns or intersecting highways, didn't think, didn't look out the window, didn't do anything. When they arrived, the bus pulled into a big parking lot behind a low, modern school building, stretched out along the top of a hill, with windows along most of the walls. The building was locked for the weekend, but the gym was open. The opposing team poured out through the broad doors as the Crisfield Warriors went in to change. This was a private school, The Acorn School. It had a team of coaches, a head of Track and two assistants. All of the competitors looked alike, except for the colors of their shorts. The Warriors wore red, the Acorn team blue. All had on white tank tops with numbers.

Bullet followed the mass of moving bodies to the field, hanging back. The oval track lay in a kind of meadow between two gentle hills. A white board fence surrounded it. From the top of a rise of land, watching people spread out over and around the field, Bullet picked out the brown rectangle that was the long jump pit, the circle from which the javelin would be thrown, the tall pole vault posts and the shorter high jump posts. A pile of white hurdles lay piled up beside the gateway to the track. A couple of long white benches were set out for spectators and equipment. The cross-country path led up through mown grass, over the opposite hill, to disappear into the sky. The sky shone deep blue. White clouds, broad and lazy, drifted across it.

Bullet stood watching. The mass broke up into smaller groups, bending and stretching in exercises. The coaches, three blue windbreakers and one red one, moved among the groups. Two officials stood by the starting line on the track, in black-and-white striped shirts and black shorts. From a distance, the competitors looked like animals turned loose into a field, guided by herdsmen into positions on the lush meadow while the officials oversaw the whole operation. From a distance, the whole scene looked ordered, designed, completed.

If he could paint, Bullet thought, this was something that would make a painting, in oil to catch the quality of color the clear air brought out. The rich green of the grass; the brown of track and pits so perfectly brown it looked like it had to be some other substance, not really earth at all, maybe gold; and the figures of the young men, lying on the grass with their fingers locked behind their necks, muscles pulling effortlessly up, or running in place with high-lifted knees: but he didn't paint, couldn't even draw, and didn't want to.

He went down the slope to find out when his events were.

The coach moved around, checking up, checking in, encouraging and advising. He handed Bullet the clipboard. On the top of the papers was a mimeographed sheet listing the order of events. Cross-country, as usual, came near the end. As always, the relay race came last. When he was a ninth grader, Bullet ran with the relay team. The coach had tried to get him to run sprints too, but he refused—he was fast enough but he didn't like running on the track, in the lines. After one season, Bullet could decide what events he would enter, and he refused to run in the relay anymore.

"Tillerman, you time the sprints," the coach told him. Bullet hung the stopwatch around his neck and moved on along the fence to stand at the hundred-meter mark. After a while, the finish tape was set up across the eight lanes of track, and he saw eight runners move into position—four pairs of blue shorts, four red. They crouched, bodies coiled into position, heads down. In unison, they raised their bodies up to rest on fingertips and toes and then—a split second later, at the sound of a blank being fired—they sprang off their marks. Bullet started the stopwatch at the same time.

Fifteen seconds later it was all over, and the eight runners were going back to their coaches to check times and hear advice. Bullet filled in the places and times for their runners: four, six, seven, eight; the times ranged from 13.1 to 14.8 seconds. The winning time was 11.9, a little kid, probably a ninth grader, skinny and fast, who headed for the finish line as if that was his only hope in the whole world.

Bullet moved up to the two hundred meter mark, halfway around the track. Two members of the Crisfield team were running both of these races, which put them at a disadvantage. But they were strong starters, which gave them some chance—in those leagues—of competing: not that day, though, the Acorn runners had been well-coached, had trained hard. Crisfield took the bottom four positions in the two hundred. Bullet wrote down the results, then moved to stand near the group by the starting line, to time the four hundred meter, once around the track. There, waiting for the gun to sound, his finger poised over the stopper, he could watch the start close up. Eight tense bodies, each in position at the far right edge of the lane, waited. The gun went, he pushed down. The runners were away.

Into the first straight they were bunched. Acorn was running that little guy again, and he pulled out ahead, legs pumping, head slewing as his shoulders swung, setting the pace fast. At the turn, about halfway around, he fell apart, dropping rapidly back, his legs loose and awkward. The three other Acorn runners started to move forward at that time. The field stretched way out. Bullet watched. Only one Crisfield runner could stay near the leading pack, and he trailed them by increasing distances. Watching, noting the strategy employed by the opponents, Bullet wondered why the Crisfield runner couldn't keep up—his legs were strong enough, he had the shoulders and chest to go with them. He marked the time across the line, 55 seconds, and then, several seconds later, the three remaining Warriors. The little guy stumbled last across the line, his face furious, ashamed.

Acorn's timer, whose long arms and legs marked him as probably a vaulter, looked over at Bullet. His eyes sparkled, then he muted his enthusiasm. "They finally decided to put some money into track," he said. "Our youngest coach—with the blond crew cut?—he ran for West Point. The eight hundred. He knows what he's doing. Tactics too." He waited for Bullet's reply.

Bullet didn't say anything, just moved off to report in. He couldn't stand these good sports types. The team had been well-trained and they ran better—why apologize? The other boy fell into step with him. "You're S. Tillerman, aren't you?"

"Yeah."

"My name's Hurley, George Hurley."

So what.

"I've heard about you. I'm pleased to meet you. I don't run cross-country."

Buzz off. Why don't you.

"You've been state champion for two years, haven't you?"

Bullet nodded, wishing the guy would get off his heels. He walked faster. He couldn't stand these guys, with their good-sport faces and rich-kid haircuts and professional quality track shoes.

"Are you going to try the Nationals this year?" Hurley asked.

"No," Bullet said, letting all of the anger that was building up out in his voice. The kid finally got the message.

Bullet entered the times and returned the stopwatch. The coach moved to the center of the track, where the long jump pitch had been dug. Bullet stayed back, at his distance.

Long jump always took a while, as jumpers were eliminated after a couple of rounds. Bullet watched the jumpers—the near sprint up the approach, the spring into the air, the midair kick to gain distance, then the heels digging into the sand to land at farthest extension. You could see in the long jump how the body worked, muscles and bones together, how the machinery was put together. You could see the muscles tense for the spring, then hang loose for a second before gathering themselves up around the bones to push forward; and finally, stretch out—extended along the length of the leg bones, and the arm bones too. All the bones with their weight and length worked with the muscles to pull the jumper's body forward. Tamer was their best long-jumper, but he was landing with his feet tucked under his knees, using his ankles to take the shock of landing. He only got a fourth and Bullet saw the coach move up to talk at him.

Bullet threw the javelin, which he didn't mind. It gave his chest and arms some warm-up, and he liked the dead stop feeling all along his skeleton as he landed on his brake foot and swung the throwing arm around, picking up the shock of the stop to add to the force behind his throw. A couple of the Crisfield throwers were disqualified for overstepping the throwing line, but Bullet never made that mistake. His reflexes were too good. He got a second with 115 feet. He guessed that none of Acorn's hot-shot coaches was a javelin man. One fifteen wouldn't even place you in most meets.

The morning went on. They ran two middle-distance races, then the four hundred meter hurdles. Bullet watched the hurdle race with some interest, leaning on the top rail of the fence, the sun warm on his head and shoulders. The Acorn team took the hurdles higher than they had to, almost doing a split in midair over the bar. They were awkward about it, and sometimes even came down on top of the hurdle, but they got height that way. The Warriors, except for Tamer, just ran over the fences, which were so low in these leagues that they looked all right. Tamer, however, approached each jump as the opponents did, but with more coordination, as if he knew what he was doing. He took a good lead, his heavy thighs moving him well for the thirty-odd yards between jumps, always taking off from his right foot with no break in stride. Bullet watched the way the left leg lifted and extended, the right leg got pulled up and folded in, but held horizontal. You landed on your left foot into a full run. Bullet could feel along his muscles how to do that. When he came to fences or obstacles in cross-country, he took them like the high jump essentially: slowing down to get into position, lifting his body up and over, then getting back into stride as quickly as possible. The hurdlers got a forward lift, really a part of the run, and their landings moved right back into stride. Leaning against the wooden rails, Bullet felt his leg muscles trying it. His legs wanted to land on the right foot; he'd have to push off with his left—that felt right.

He skipped the pole vault, sitting aside on the grassy hillside watching the sky instead. It was past noon, but nobody would be hungry until the meet was finished. They'd stop at the Dairy Queen on the way back, to stoke up on hamburgers and milkshakes. Bullet let the feeling of the hurdlers' jumps run down his legs, trying to get from his arms what they would be doing. He'd seen hurdlers like this before, he thought, but he'd never connected how he might use their approach. He wondered why, but only in passing. The only way to see if it worked was to try it, and it was a waste of time to think about why he hadn't thought to try it before.

The cross-country started off flat, then went up a long, slow rise. Bullet took the hill smoothly, steadily, every stride increasing the lead he'd gotten at the start. Over the top of the hill, taking the down-slope as steadily and smoothly, he smiled to himself: it promised to be a lovely run, all three miles of it, and whoever thought to start it off with a hill would surely have some interesting ideas about how to continue it. The course branched off to the right, for its two-and-a-half-mile loop. Bullet ran, fast. He kept his eyes on the path ahead. They'd mark the course if it diverged. Fields and a tumbled-down rail fence—he had to do some quick shuffling to get his left foot in position for the jump, and he whanged that ankle against the top rail of the fence landing; but when he came down onto his right foot and strode off without hesitation, he knew the technique would suit him. Splashing through a broad shallow creek, the water icy, his foot slipped along the side of a buried rock and he went down. He turned the fall into a start, pushed himself up off his ankles, came dripping and muddy out of the water and ran. The markers took him straight across a field of tomatoes. The dessicated vines hung on tipi-shaped skeletons. He dodged around those that came into his straight line, feeling his weight shift, shoulder to ankle, as he cut them as close as possible. Running fast. Arms pumping. Eyes on the path ahead.

He slid down into a gulley, scrambled up the far side over fallen tree limbs and emerged into a stand of pines, an island of trees between pastures. A few milk cows grazed in the field he ran past, beyond a barbed wire fence. The uneven ground rolled under his feet. The muscles across his back pulled and released, smooth as waves on the water. Another stand of pines and an unexpected fence, the red ribbons tied on either end. The tumbled wood stuck up at odd angles with a few nails coming out. It was low enough to run over, almost, without any change of pace, but he wanted to work on the hurdling jump. He approached the low obstacle at a dead run, pushing himself off with his left foot, reaching out with the right, remembering how the hurdlers had looked. He almost cleared it; something hooked his left calf, down to the ankle. Landing, he absorbed his forward motion with his right leg and brought his left knee up, forward, into the steady pace of running fast.

When the paths rejoined, Bullet increased his speed—up two beats. He pushed it up the slope, then relaxed down the opposite side, careful not to let the descent upset his pace or his balance, which was the danger in a downslope, especially at the end of the course. At the final stretch he ran full out, knees high, chest high, and didn't stop until he was well beyond the crowd at the finish. He stood straight, with his back to them looking over the oval track, breathing deeply. A good run.

The coach came over to congratulate him and tell him his time. Bullet nodded, wiping sweat away from his eyes. He went back to stand near the finish line. The coach said something to him, but he didn't hear it clearly. "Your leg," the coach repeated.

Bullet looked down. Blood was swelling out of a long cut on his left leg, the way blood did just before it started to really clot. His lower calf was streaked with dried blood. He went over to wrap a gauze bandage around it—one of the nails probably. Not too deep, but it shouldn't have happened. You could expect bruises and surface lacerations on a good, tough course, but not a cut that would strip off a flap of skin. He tied off the gauze and drifted over to where the three blue windbreakers stood in a line, the coaches watching the top of the hill to see who would appear.

The blond one spoke in a low voice. "You didn't expect to beat him, did you?"

"I'd like to have come a little closer." The head coach spoke crossly. "It's been over three minutes, and we've trained them on this course."

"The kid's a natural," the blond answered, moving his head to look at the man the was talking to, which brought Bullet into his line of vision. "Speak of the devil," he said. He was tall, muscular and held himself with military erectness. "Nice race, Tillerman. I was just saying, I'd trade my right arm for the chance to give you some real training."

Bullet's chin went up as he clamped down on a surge of pride. A compliment was only worth what the man who paid it was worth, and he had no reason to value this guy. Who did he think he was, anyway? Thinking because he was full-grown and had run himself . . . It made Bullet angry, as if he needed training, as if he'd want this guy to train him anyway. "You've got a fence with protruding nails on the course."

"We know our own course." The blue eyes challenged him.

"That's illegal."

The guy eyeballed him. "Is it?" he said. "Are you complaining?"

Bullet stared right back at him. *What do you think?* After some long seconds, he walked away. He didn't know what the subject of the low conversation behind him was, and he didn't care.

A figure in blue shorts staggered to the top of the hill and began an awkward descent, legs too stiff. Another figure in blue crested, then a bunch, mostly blue with one red. They straggled down the hillside, not even on the path. The leader tripped over his own misplaced feet, rolled and stopped, stretched out. It took him a few seconds to get up again, and in that time he was overtaken by the man behind him. Coming down the hillside, one of the grouped runners pulled ahead, the guy in red, as if the sight of the finish gave him the strength to take another try. It was, from the color and size of him, Tamer. He didn't hurry the downhill and moved into the final stretch still running. There were four runners on the stretch, strung out and moving without any coordination, arms loose, eyes a little wild, mouths open, stride uneven. Tamer was too slow to catch them up, but he had his stride. As he came closer, Bullet could see the muscles at his neck straining, and the bunching of those along his thighs. His whole body was wet with sweat, so that his skin shone as if it had been oiled and his tank top stuck to his torso, showing where the ribcage underneath was wrapped around and around with bandages.

As the runners crossed the finish line, they fell down onto their hands and knees. The three Acorn coaches moved over to get them out of the way, to pull them to the back of the crowd. There they left them, crouched on all fours. Tamer ran himself out of the way, as if his body was a machine running down. He fell onto the grass and lay there. The coach moved over to talk to him, then called to Bullet. "Get a water bottle." The coach went back to wait at the finish line. Bullet stood over Tamer, the plastic bottle in his hand. The big back heaved.

"You feel okay?" Bullet asked. Sometimes athletes did bust a blood vessel, or have a heart attack, depending on the kind of strain they put themselves under. Young, apparently healthy guys.

"I feel like shit," the muffled voice answered. Tamer rolled over onto his back. He opened his dark eyes. "Tillerman. I should have known." He closed his eyes.

When he opened them again, it was to make an accusation: "You white bastard, you knew it would be harder than the practice course." Lying flat, he clenched his fists against his hips. "And *he* wouldn't tell us how bad it would be because then we wouldn't sign up, and if he didn't have the runners he couldn't put you in the field." He looked up at Bullet, his anger controlled. "It's been a long time since Whitey outfigured me."

Bullet shrugged. It wasn't his problem. He dropped the bottle onto the ground by Tamer's arm. Tamer sat up and sipped from the straw.

"You knew, didn't you? Save your breath, Whitey; I know you knew how bad it would be in a race. My question is, did you know the rest of us didn't?"

Bullet considered not answering, then decided to. "People seem to think if they can run a practice they can run a race."

"Born jackasses," Tamer said, glaring up at Bullet.

You're no better.

"Anyway, I finished," Tamer said.

"Usually nobody does the first time," Bullet allowed him; it was the simple truth.

"Did you fall?" There was no sympathy in the question, or in the glance at his leg.

"A nail on one of those fences." Blood was oozing through the gauze again. He'd have to rewrap it.

"They gave me no trouble," the guy announced. "No trouble a-tall. How about leaving me be, Tillerman. I don't much like your company."

Bullet almost grinned. *Suits me.* He went to rebandage his leg.

CHAPTER 10

Bullet sat alone on the way back, across from the coach. Behind him, he heard the voices reassuring themselves that they hadn't done too badly, had they? Justifying their poor performances to one another, envying the setup at Acorn, declaring that they could look just as good, if, and if, and if. *If you'd work at it, work for it,* Bullet thought. Then, after they had eaten, the voices got louder, relieved that the meet was behind them and able to forget exactly how it had gone. Bullet stayed out of it. He wasn't about to mess with them, people who made excuses for themselves. That kept him pretty much alone, he knew; it marked one of the differences. He had his own life in his own hands, that was the difference. Not perfectly in his own hands, not entirely, he wasn't a fool and he knew that wasn't possible. But he ran himself. They didn't, simple as that; they didn't and they knew he did, and they admired him for it and disliked him. Too bad. Maybe. Maybe they'd grow up some time. He didn't care: that had nothing to do with him. He was his own business, he knew what he wanted and whenever he could he went for that. When he couldn't—like the draft—he did what he had to and no more, like school. Besides, he wasn't so sure he'd mind the army. Talk about natural habitats, he thought to himself, feeling the smile that washed over his features. He'd decide about that too, sometime, and he knew that when he'd decided he could count on himself to act out his own decisions.

Opposite him, as they went alongside Cambridge, through Salisbury, turned southwest to head back to Crisfield, the motor of the bus grinding loudly, the coach sat silent in his seat. He sat silent, but not quiet—he shifted his weight, he banged occasionally with his fist on his thigh, he put his chin in his hand and stared out the window, thinking so hard you could almost hear the sound of gears even over the motor. Bullet could figure out what he was thinking. This was his third year on the track team, he'd been at two other opening meets. The coach was thinking how much better *this* first meet was than earlier years. He was thinking that victory might be within reach, or if not victory then at least honorable defeat. He was figuring out some kind of pep talk for the end of the trip, before they got off the bus, to get everyone working harder, trying harder.

When the bus nosed up to the water's edge in Crisfield and the engine fell silent, the coach stood up at the front, clipboard in his hand. "Okay. I know some of you—most of you—are thinking we didn't do so hot today," he called down the length of the bus. Groans and brief sarcastic bursts of laughter answered him.

"Okay. I know. But I know something you smart guys don't. I've never had a team look so good the first time out. That's God's truth."

A surprised silence answered him.

"God's truth," the coach repeated.

Rumbles of pleasure went along the bus behind Bullet. "Then last year must of been really bad," somebody said.

"We're gonna work," the coach announced. "We're gonna work harder than you thought you could. And here's why: because I think we can get somewhere. Now listen up good to this, because you're not gonna hear me say it again—all you're gonna hear from me is criticism and yelling from now on—so here's your one chance to hear what it's about."

They sat alert.

"You're good enough. All of you. Not just the old streamlined wonder"—he lifted a hand from the back of the seat to indicate Bullet—"but everyone. I'll be expecting you to do us proud, every one of you. Whaddayou say?"

Somebody called out, "Sounds okay to me, Coach." Others echoed, "Yeah. Me too."

"Let's hear it louder," the coach called. "Do you say okay?"

"Okay!" they roared.

He stood back to let them pour out of the bus and into the waiting cars. He and Bullet got off last. The bus was driving off as they got into the coach's car. The coach inserted his keys and sat for a minute, letting the motor warm up, looking out over the harbor where low workboats rocked at their moorings under late-afternoon sunlight. "You too, Tillerman."

I always run my best.

The coach backed the car around and headed out of town.

"There's some possibility there this year. I'll tell you." He stopped at an intersection by a rundown Victorian house with two unmatched towers that looked out over the street with broken windows. "It would feel good to show them."

Show who? Bullet wondered.

"They slap the job on me, knowing I can't refuse, then don't give me anything for supplies, or proper equipment—nothing, barely any upkeep even. If I had the kind of staff we saw today, and equipment, and space . . . I mean, what do I know about hurdling, or cross-country?"

Not much, Bullet agreed.

"I been a laughing stock," the coach said, slapping on the

wheel with the palm of his hand. "But this year . . . I don't expect to win, or anything, but how'd you like to look good at the state championships this year? How would that feel? That would feel pretty good, wouldn't it."

Bullet shrugged. He came in first, that was what he did. But he guessed the coach might prefer the whole team to do better.

"So I got a favor to ask you, kid. Not a big one. I want you to train Shipp in cross-country, okay?" He looked over at Bullet.

Bullet shook his head.

"Sure you can," the coach told him. "And he's got guts—he wasn't even supposed to run today, his *wife* called me up, a wife, can you believe it? I'll never understand those people; not in a hundred years. The guy's in high school. Doctor said, she told me, take it easy for a week. But you saw him. He hasn't got your talent, I know that. But he's got guts. And that counts for a lot, doesn't it?"

Bullet didn't say anything.

The coach pulled over by the Tillermans' mailbox. "Don't get out. You'll do it, won't you?"

"No," Bullet said.

Silence greeted this remark. Then, "This is no time for jokes, Tillerman."

Bullet didn't say anything. He waited. He made his own decisions and stood by them; he played by his own rules. The coach knew that.

"Why not?" the coach asked.

"He's colored."

"So what? What's that got to do with anything? Some of them are great athletes, you got to respect that."

No, Bullet didn't, he didn't see how that had anything to do with the point in question.

"This is the team we're talking about."

"I don't mix," Bullet said.

"You're telling me you won't work with him, because he's a Negro?"

That's right.

"You're on the team. That's mixing."

I run cross-country.

"Tillerman, I'm telling you to train him. Whatever you happen to feel in that little pea brain of yours. It's an order. You hear me?"

"No," Bullet said.

"You won't? You're telling me you won't? Won't you?"

"No," Bullet repeated patiently.

The coach took a deep breath. "Then as of now, as of this minute"—he spat out the words—"you are off the team. And not running. I don't need any swellheaded prima donna, a *bald* prima donna, who doesn't play on the team. Who can't take orders. Damn your eyes, Tillerman, I've let you be, let you go, given you what you wanted. What's with you?"

Bullet got out of the car. He jogged up the rutted driveway between the two fields. He was about halfway along when he heard the car start off with a squealing of rubber. And he was angry, angry at being backed into a corner like that and then the coach throwing him off the team—as if he cared about that. He made his own decisions and he'd never complained about the price he paid. He was willing to pay this price too. He didn't have to run with the team, the coach could suit himself about that. That was the coach's problem. But nobody was going to tell Bullet how to run his life, nobody was going to make him do something he didn't want to because they wanted him to. He didn't like people trying that trick on him.

Bullet didn't go after the coloreds, he wasn't out to get them; he just kept clear. He didn't mix. He didn't like them, didn't like anything about them, the way they looked or talked, the things they did, the music they played or the way they danced, the way their minds worked. . . . He didn't like much of anyone, come to that, but he didn't like coloreds more than he didn't like other people. Bullet figured he was allowed his prejudice. Nobody had the right to take that away from him, nobody was going to do that to him.

He had time on his hands now. Now that he no longer had practice, he often stopped by Patrice's on his way home. Patrice didn't expect to see him, didn't act surprised. Bullet didn't say much, just sat on an upturned hull and watched Patrice work over the fourteen-footer. He'd removed all of the curved floorboards and was sanding down the sloping sides to smooth, bare wood. "I could sand," Bullet offered.

Patrice said no. "You don't have the patience, you don't have the touch."

"I bet I could get the transom off for you."

"Yes, that you can, please," Patrice said. He didn't watch as Bullet wrested loose the cracked pieces of wood, hammering at them to work them free.

"I could teach you to do this," Patrice offered, bent over the tedious job. "If you would like."

"No, thanks. Will you be able to get the oak?"

"Of course. The question you want to ask is, will I be able to get it at a price I like. That"—he forestalled Bullet's question—"I do not yet know." And he was off, talking about differences in lumber yards, about the men who ran them and worked in them. Bullet listened, easy with Patrice because Patrice was easy, at ease, an easy man.

If Patrice wasn't there, or if Bullet felt like it, he went straight home and took his twenty-two out, to get his eye back. He shot at crows, squirrels, rabbits, whatever he saw as he moved through the woods beyond the fields, or the pines between them. Once he got the Smith and Wesson, once the season opened, he could work on targeting. For the time, he worked on reflexes. He moved quiet and slow through the shady sparse woods, using his peripheral vision, alert to any movement. You caught movement and had to get the gun up, the shot off, before the creature moved away. It took patience and constant alertness—it was an instant reaction he was working for. Every now and again he would run into OD, or she would sometimes follow him out; but she was useless. She moved clumsily through the underbrush, warning everything. He'd throw a branch at her, or kick her. At least she didn't bark, that was something.

He did get one crow, which tumbled off the branch and into a bush with a squawk. Not thinking, he shot an egret—his eye caught by the flash of white moving up from the bank, his reaction instinctive. The bird slid down the air with one wing dragging. Bullet didn't think it would survive.

And he ran, every evening, the ten-mile course. He even ran it the drizzly evening after their first day of oystering, when his shoulders and the backs of his legs felt like they'd been tied up in knots. Six hours of leaning over the side of the boat with his arms stretched out. Six hours of forcing the tongs at the end of their long handles down into the muddy bottom. The hard work came after that, pulling the handles apart to close the teeth and hauling them straight up, hand over hand, while you leaned out over the water to keep them vertical. At least he and Patrice took shifts on that. It wasn't grip or dexterity you needed for oysters. All you needed was strength and stamina. Running, that first evening, Bullet felt the knotted muscles pulling loose, each separate strand of muscle forced to stretch out and trying to snap back into the knot.

After the first weekend, a couple of people spoke to him about dropping track. Jim, with Ted Bayson at his back, congratulated Bullet on getting out of a losing situation.

"I wasn't losing," Bullet said.

"Okay, okay." Jim backed off. "I was just wondering if you'd like to try football. We wouldn't mind that. We're two, one and zero so far."

Bullet shook his head.

A couple of track people tried to get him to come back. "We don't have much of a chance without you."

"Chance for what?"

"Getting to the state championships. Hell, we don't have any chance without you."

Bullet shrugged.

"But what's your beef?"

Cheryl's reaction was to say maybe Bullet was starting to grow up and attend to what was important; but after Jackson found out why he wasn't doing track—how, Bullet didn't know—they also demanded, "What's your beef? You're cutting off your nose to spite your face, man."

Bullet didn't care. He wasn't interested in talking, and what did they know anyway—thinking if the words came out right then everything was in control.

"But how can you not run?" Tommy asked him. "I saw you a couple of times last year. You're terrific. How can you give that up?"

They apparently thought he'd given it up, and they didn't understand anything. They thought they understood, but he'd always known better.

"I run," he told them.

They didn't have words to wrap around that statement, so they let him be.

He ran because it was what he did, what he was. He didn't run to win races, or to beat anybody. He ran because his body was built for it. He ran for himself. Simple as that.

CHAPTER 11

Bullet moved along through the big doors with everybody else. Some of them funneled off to go get into the school buses. A group went on around to the student parking lot. A few, mostly younger kids, had bikes waiting in the racks by the door. Bullet drifted down the walk toward the road. It wasn't raining, for a change; it had been raining steadily for the last four days, a chilly, slanting fall rain that knocked the leaves off the trees and turned the ground into mud patches. The meet that weekend would have been run in the rain, which was always gruelling. Bullet had run his daily ten miles, but that wasn't as hard because he knew it too well. He glanced at a silver sports car pulled up alongside the curb, a low-slung convertible, top down, with a long hood swept over its motor. It was the kind of car that looked like it was doing ninety when it was standing still. A redhead sat behind the wheel, smoking. A man lounged against the hood. Bullet didn't know how the track team had done in the meet. He didn't ask and nobody told him.

The sun shone, weak and watery, but still sunshine. He thought about going to Patrice's. There'd probably be something he could do, and Patrice would feed him and invite him for supper too. He was pretty sick of his own cooking. He thought about stopping at Tydings' for a steak, but he didn't have a meet. He thought he'd go back home, then, and put in a couple of hours hunting. Rabbits didn't come out until later in the day, but if he could bag a couple of rabbits he could probably stew them, or something. His mother kept him stocked with canned goods, soups and spaghetti and hash, but it had been a few weeks now and he was pretty sick of everything there. He thought he would drop in on Patrice after all—the rain had kept them shorebound that weekend. Patrice had called on Saturday, surprised to hear Bullet answer the phone, to say his joints couldn't take the weather so they wouldn't be going out Sunday.

There was something familiar about the figure lounging against the sports car, jeans low on narrow hips—Frank. Frank Verricker. Bullet strode over to greet him, with a quick glance at the redhead: Would Liza dye her hair? Or smoke?

"Frank?" he said.

The narrow face turned to him, eyes laughing. It wasn't Liza anyway, which explained the hair. "Hey, kid. I told Honey you'd find me. How've you been? Surprised to see me?"

"Well, yeah," Bullet said. "Of course." Frank looked the same, light eyes, thick, dark hair, the body long, lean.

"Good thing you saw me. I wouldn't have recognized you," Frank said. "What's it been, four years? Seven? Why'd you shave your head? You aren't a monk or something, are you?"

Bullet grinned, shook his head, rubbed his hand over the top of it.

"What are you now, five-eleven? About one sixty, one seventy? You look strong, kid."

"Frankie." The woman called attention to herself.

Frank turned to introduce her. "Honey—meet my man, Bullet, a very old friend. Bullet, meet Honey, a recent acquaintance."

"Hi," Bullet said.

"Hi there." She smiled up at him. She had a cat face. Her glossy red hair was arranged in waves around her head. Makeup made her green eyes look larger, lipstick made her little mouth shine. She had a scarf around her shoulders and a white blouse that opened low in the front and bright red silk trousers. Her nails were long and as pink as her lips. She smiled at him like she really liked him. "We drove six hours to see you, you know. You must be somebody special."

What was he supposed to say to that? He didn't much like the way she was looking at him, either. He turned to Frank.

"All the way down from Baltimore," Frank said. "What do you think of her?" he asked Bullet.

Bullet didn't know how to answer.

"The car, kid."

"Is it yours?"

"What do you think?"

"I think I'd believe anything," Bullet said. "You could have borrowed it, or rented it, maybe stolen it. I admit, I can't imagine you bought it. Did you win it in a card game?"

Honey chuckled.

"You always were a lippy kid. You know what she is? An XKE, she'll hit one fifty without even trying hard. Want to go for a spin?"

The car had two low seats, both covered in black leather. Behind the seats was a narrow space, about big enough for a large suitcase. "Where would I sit?"

"Honey can squeeze herself into the tonneau, can't you?"

"Sure. I'm used to tight corners."

She slid out from behind the wheel and stepped into the back of the car, slipped down into the narrow space and smiled at Bullet: "See?" Bullet got into the front seat and Frank got behind the wheel. The key chain had a wooden honey pot, with HONEY painted on it. Frank turned on the motor and turned to grin at Bullet. "Watch this."

He gunned the motor, slipped the car into first, took off with a squeal of tires and shifted quickly into second. “Whaddaya think of that, kid?” Frank asked, above the smooth sound of the motor. Bullet nodded his head. Frank had such a good time, doing everything—anything was fun when Frank was around.

They took the highway out of town, a smooth, flat, two-lane road. The wind whipped around their heads. The speedometer kept moving—fifty-five, sixty, seventy, seventy-five, eighty-five. Bullet felt the machine moving under him, all of its parts in perfect synchronization, running smooth. Honey reached over to put her hand on Frank’s shoulder. It rested there, its pink nails bright against the faded denim jacket. Frank turned his head to kiss it, briefly, his eyes still on the road ahead. The fingers tightened. “Okay, okay,” he said, and the speedometer began to slide down, more slowly than it had climbed up. At forty he swung the car around in a U-turn. The back fishtailed slightly and he gunned it back into control. “Some car, hunh, kid?” he asked. Bullet nodded.

They pulled off at a roadhouse, the Lazy-B, where a few cars were already parked in the oystershell lot. Frank turned around to face his passengers. “We could pick up a couple of six-packs or we can go in. Any preferences?”

Honey pulled herself up to sit on the trunk. She unwrapped the scarf from her head. “How grungy is it?”

“It’s been years, but it wasn’t too bad. There’s a jukebox, all the golden oldies. People start coming in around five, it gets lively—lively for around here, that is. There’s a dance floor.”

“I’m underage,” Bullet said.

“He doesn’t care about that,” Honey reassured him. “He doesn’t even have a driver’s license, do you, Frankie?”

“You been going through my wallet?”

"Why would I do that when I know it's empty? It was just a guess, a smart guess—to show I know my man."

Frank subsided.

"Besides," Honey told Bullet, "you look old enough. With your head shaved and all. You look handsome enough. I don't mind being seen with you, not at all. And Frankie says you're something else. Let's go ahead in."

"Fine by me," Bullet agreed.

Inside, there were two rooms, one with a bar and bar stools, one with booths and an open dance floor. A couple of men sat at the bar. Nobody was in the other room. Frank led them into it and to a corner booth. He slid in first and Honey sat beside him. Bullet sat opposite. He looked around the room—it was paneled in dark wood and hung with wild west pictures, wild west wanted posters, branding irons, a few Stetsons and a sign that said, "Park your pistol with the lady, pardner." Over the two bathroom doors, one labeled Bulls, the other Heifers, hung the gatepost to a ranch, the Lazy-B, with its brand—a capital B lying on its back on rockers—in the center. Fake, it was the fakest place Bullet had ever seen.

Against the back wall was a jukebox, with fluorescent colors running all around it, chasing each other. Overhead, wagon wheels suspended from the ceiling held lights.

"I'm gonna see what songs they have," Honey said. "Order me a stinger, will you, Frankie? You'll be driving back, no problem." She moved over to study the jukebox, her purse hanging from her shoulder.

Frank followed her with his eyes. "What do you think of her, kid?"

Bullet didn't say anything.

"She's a looker, isn't she?"

"Yeah."

The bartender came over. "What'll you have?" Frank asked Bullet, who ordered ginger ale. Frank ordered two draft beers for himself, and "A stinger for the lady. The lady's paying. You don't drink?" he asked Bullet.

"Naw."

"Why not? Can't you handle it?"

"It tastes bad."

Frank laughed. "We call that an acquired taste, right, kid? You haven't changed, you always did shoot from the hip."

"What're you doing here anyway?" Bullet asked. Their drinks came and he pulled the straw out of his glass before lifting it.

"I ran out of luck. Would you believe that three days ago I could put my hand into my pocket and pull out a couple of thousand dollars? Well, that's gone now, some New York sharper has my money in his pocket now. Bad luck. Sob sob." Frank grinned at Bullet over the top of his glass. "So, I'm looking for a berth, and a friend of mine knows of one I can probably get, but there were a couple of days to kill. Honey had this car." He moved over to give her room as she returned. The jukebox burst into song. "It stopped raining, and we felt like a drive. Right, doll?"

"I'm always ready for a trip," she smiled.

"You *are* a trip. Anyway, so here we are," Frank said. "You must be in high school by now, kid. Are you going to finish?"

"Why not?"

"How the hell would I know why not?" Frank asked. "I haven't seen you for years. Maybe you got thrown out? Maybe picked up by some talent scout to understudy Yul Brynner. I'm asking to find out. You got any plans?"

"They'll draft him," Honey said.

"I don't mind," Bullet told her.

"And after that? If you're still in one piece?" Frank asked.

"That depends," Bullet said.

"I told you he was close-mouthed, didn't I," Frank remarked to Honey.

He didn't answer that, but asked instead, "What is it, did you grow up around here or something? Is that how come you wanted to come back and find Bullet?" She didn't ask it like she cared about the answer, but she was too casual to fool Bullet.

Frank winked at him. "I didn't grow up around here. Did I, Bullet?"

"Nope."

This frustrated her. "Where *did* you grow up then?"

"Here and there, I told you that."

"That doesn't tell me anything. Bullet? Do you know?"

"No, ma'am, I don't," Bullet said.

"Don't ma'am me, I'm not that old. I'm probably no more than a year or two older than you are."

Frank laughed into his beer.

"Honestly, Frank Tompkins, I don't believe there's a word of truth in you."

Frank shrugged. "You want to leave, you can go ahead. My man Bullet will get me back to Baltimore. Won't you?"

Bullet didn't say anything. He knew Frank wasn't the kind of man you ever lent money to, not if you expected to see it again.

"I'm not angry, Frankie, you know that. I don't want to leave. I don't care, whatever you want to tell, I don't need to know any more than I do. You know that. I know the really important stuff. Anyway, I want to dance. Let's dance, okay?"

"Not now, doll. I want to talk to Bullet here." He looked at Bullet, his expression amused by Honey's antics, his eyes inviting Bullet to join in the joke. "So, anyway, kid, how's your family?"

"About the same."

"I'm sorry to hear that." Frank grinned.

"Yeah." Bullet grinned back.

"I was sort of hoping your old man might have kicked off. Oh well. Sob sob, right?" Frank lifted his glass and drank, the other arm around Honey. The room began to fill up with people, sitting at the booths, standing around the jukebox, men and women. Frank raised his hand to get the bartender's attention and ordered another round of drinks.

"What about you?" Bullet asked. "What have you been doing? Where have you been?"

"Where haven't I been," Frank told him. "Japan, Taiwan, Australia—I could live in Australia, that's one big country. Kuwait, J'burg, Vancouver. I've been all around the world, all the hell around it, crossways and top to bottom. Pineapples, bananas, TV components, copra, copper, oil, bauxite. You name it. The big money's in oil, of course—I spent some time on the run between New Orleans and Panama. That's what I do when I need money fast. But—my God it gets through to you."

Honey got up and went into the other room, her drink in her hand. Frank watched her go.

"Those old tubs—I mean, kid, here are these derelict tankers filled with crude oil, right? The stuff could go up any minute. Every time you light a cigarette, you could blow it. They're coming apart at the seams, and fumes all over the place. I used to sleep out on deck—it made me sick at my stomach to spend time in the crew's quarters, the smell of oil. Besides, I figured—if she blew, I might just go flying clear, I'd have a chance at least. I couldn't sleep cooped up down there, knowing that if something happened I'd be trapped, like some—I dunno, some rabbit down a hole or something. Those engines are held together with string and bubble gum—and old, like some Humphrey Bogart movie. I worked with one guy, he had a scar right across his waist, just above the navel—a real scar, like some leather belt. He got caught by a boiler blowout. He was lucky he was moving when it hit him. If he'd been standing still it would have just cut him in half, the steam. Well, that's why the oilers pay the way they do. And my nerves can hold up for a couple of runs. But only if I'm desperate for funds."

Frank's eyes watched Honey come back from the bar with a man in tow and join the dancers. "I like the Pacific best." The music was so loud, Bullet had to lean forward to hear what he was saying. "I like them all, but the Pacific is the best. Mile after rolling mile of it, and every now and then you stumble on an island. Beaches and mountains and a sweet wind. . . . If I live old enough, I'm going to retire to one of those islands. The way the waves break on the reefs and spread up onto the sand . . . On the Pacific, you're riding those big waves, day after day after day."

Honey stopped by to ask Frank to dance again and he said, "Not yet, doll, lay off a little." She went back to the dance floor with another man, younger than the first.

"You know, kid, you ought to ask her to dance, it would be polite," Frank said. Then he winked, hesitated, grinned, demanded: "Aren't you even going to *ask* about Liza?"

CHAPTER 12

Well," Bullet said, after a while.

"Well what?"

"Well, no."

The light eyes assessed him. "Hey, you ought to understand this, Honey's not mine. Somebody else picks up the tab for her. I couldn't afford Honey, the way she spends. My god, kid, you've seen that car. You know what those cars cost? But Honey's fun to be with, she can be pretty sharp. Say what you will about Liza, sharp she isn't."

The room around them was getting crowded, with people sitting and people dancing, with music and voices, with cigarette smoke rising up through the pale light from the wagon wheels suspended overhead.

"So anyway," Frank said, leaning back, emptying his glass, smiling at Bullet, "what do you think of this place?"

Bullet shrugged. He didn't think much of it.

"This was our place, Liza's and mine. This was our table. I used to meet her, just like I did you today, waiting outside that brick prison."

"I never knew that."

"Nobody knew. I told her it had to be a secret. Well, she was so young when I first saw her—and she's a looker, whatever else you say about her. I asked her to promise me not to tell, and you know how Liza is, when she makes a promise she keeps it. So we'd come on over here. Nobody cared how old she was so long as she didn't order drinks, and she didn't. We'd dance. I tell you, kid, she's the only one I ever couldn't just walk away from. And forget. Isn't that funny? I don't know why, she's not *that* good-looking. I just kept coming back, sometimes a matter of weeks, sometimes months, once it was over a year—whenever I was in Baltimore I'd just keep coming on back. She was always there. She never minded. Say what you will about her, she's got a heart of gold."

"Who does?" Honey asked, sliding in close beside Frank.

"Time for another round, don't you think?" Frank asked, taking her hand.

"Sure, but you're not going to change the subject on me like that. I know you weren't talking about me, on account of I do not have a heart of gold. That's not my big attraction."

"The kid's sister." Frank waved at the bartender.

"She's the one you're married to?"

"Well," Frank said, "what can I say?" He grinned at Bullet.

You can say yes or no, Bullet thought, then he shrugged. Nothing to do with him.

"Hey, handsome, how about a dance?" Honey asked him. "Would you do that?"

"I don't know how."

"No kidding? Really? I guess it's time you learned then, hunh? Or how you going to show the girls your stuff. Come on, I'll teach you."

He followed her out onto the dance floor. She led him into the center, winding among couples, making sure he stayed with her by holding on to his hand. She knew he didn't much want to dance, knew he would have slipped away if he could have. In the midst of the slowly moving couples, she turned to look up at him. She told him where to put his right hand and held out her right hand for him to take with his left. "Then you just kind of move your feet to the rhythm, and I follow your lead." Her face laughed up at him. Bullet tried a couple of steps, feeling clumsy because of having to move her body around too. She giggled. He let her go.

"Hey, don't get angry," she said, opening her eyes big and wide and looking up at him to make him feel taller than he was. "Look, it's like this—" She demonstrated a sliding step, holding on to his left hand. She had, he saw, green powder on her eyelids, and her eyebrows had been painted into an arc they didn't naturally grow in: this close, he could see how she had layered on her makeup, he could almost pick off the coatings of mascara on her eyelashes. Liza's hair flowed like a river down her back, a honey-colored river; her eyes were hazel but her lashes were thick and dark; he could almost hear her, deep inside his head, singing in her honey-colored voice, "Will there be any stars, any stars in my crown." Bullet looked down at Honey's bright hair, smelled her dusty perfume and leaned back, away.

The metallic voice on the jukebox continued singing, ". . . and while they were dancing, my friend stole my darling from me."

Step, slide, step, slide. Bullet looked around at the other couples, some so close to each other they were just rocking from side to side, not moving around at all: *How long does this last?*

"You're Frankie's old friend," Honey teased him. "You going to steal me away?"

"No," Bullet said quickly. A flicker of anger went across her face, but she giggled at him as if he had said something funny.

"Tell me about your sister," she said. "You know, what she's like and all."

Why.

"Is she pretty? I guess probably, or she was, anyway; that's the kind of girl Frankie goes for. He told me how she won't give him a divorce, even though he hasn't been near her for three years or more . . . but you're her brother, you know all that already. I guess she's the homebody type, is she? Or is afraid to try it on her own so she needs the security of the wedding band on her finger."

I wouldn't know.

"But you ought to tell her— Oh, not about me, he's come around a few times on shore leave but he won't be coming back again, I bet. And if he does, I don't think I'll want to see him."

Why are you talking to me about this.

"Frankie's fun . . . for a while . . . but not what a girl wants to attach herself to, if you take my meaning."

And I don't want to.

"Fun is okay—and he really is fun—but—" She laughed happily, remembering. Bullet was waiting for the record to end. "He asked me if I was married. He told me right away that he was. I don't know, how could I resist him?"

Bullet didn't know, or care.

"But she shouldn't try to keep him tied down, she'll never be able to do it. And it's not as if there are any children. Speaking as a woman, I don't think I'd like to be married to him. I don't think he'd make much of a husband . . ." She leaned her head back and looked at Bullet's face. She decided to change the subject. "How about you, do you have a girlfriend?"

Bullet just looked at her. Step, slide, and the woman on the record wailing away behind him.

Then Frank was there beside him, the record ended, and Bullet stepped back, relieved. But Frank caught him by the wrist and caught Honey by the wrist. "I just invested my last two quarters. They've got everything on this jukebox, wait'll you hear—"

The couples waited around them, and then a drawling voice announced a square dance. "Pick your partners, podnuhs, and get yourselves ready," a hearty nasal voice announced. Voices around the dance floor groaned, laughed. Frank maneuvered five people into a group around them. He picked out a plump, middle-aged woman for Bullet to dance with, telling her, "He's never done this, but you look like you know how to enjoy yourself."

"You're right about that, young man," she told him, pleased.

Bullet stood where he was supposed to. "Stamp your feet, kid," Frank called across to him. "Clap your hands. Look alive."

The dance floor was made of squares of red linoleum, with brands painted on them. It held two other squares of dancers as well as their own and was encircled by a crowd that watched and clapped in time to the music. Fiddles and banjos played away on the jukebox. "Allemande left," the caller sang out, and their square began a hand-over-hand circling, which the other squares were doing too. After a couple of false starts, Bullet got the hang of it. This was more like it, this was dancing that used your whole body, where you moved with the music. He went around the circle and then, a few seconds after everybody else, turned around to go hand-over-hand in the opposite direction. All the faces he passed were smiling at him. Behind him he could hear the rhythmic clapping of the people watching, and an occasional "Waa-hoo!" They did do-si-do's, and a step where you crossed to the middle of the square, backed three times around the girl opposite, then skipped backward to your own place. While the other couples were crossing you stood stamping your foot, clapping your hands. People sometimes backed into each other and laughed.

The record ended with a promenade, where all the squares lined up by couples, clasped hands overhead to form an arch and then—one after the other, like a snake turning inside out in its skin—each couple ran through the tunnel of raised arms, becoming part of the archway at the end. Everybody stood clapping and waa-hooing and smiling.

"Now that's the way it's supposed to be," Bullet's partner said. "I thank you for the dance, young man." She was red in the face and her cheeks got round as apples when she smiled.

"I liked it," Bullet told her, telling the truth. She had danced nimbly on her round legs, skipping, kicking up her heels. "I enjoyed that." They shook hands and parted.

Somebody had claimed Honey for the next dance, and Frank led Bullet back to the booth. There he began on another glass of beer. "That old jukebox hasn't changed, not one single record, since I first put money into it. That was ten years, can you believe it?"

Bullet was feeling pretty good. He always did enjoy himself with Frank.

"What do you think, kid, isn't this a great place? I mean, where else can you get a square dance going, just by dropping a couple of quarters into a slot. You know"—his eyes were pointing at Bullet, but they weren't seeing him—"the first dance floor was built by a Greek. Daedalus, and he's the same guy who made wings to get out of prison, him and his kid, they were both locked up. In Crete, at Knossos, that's where." Frank listened to himself speaking. "Now why do I remember that? Isn't it incredible, what your brain remembers? Where would I run across a useless fact like that?"

"You're asking me?" Bullet asked.

Frank grinned and combed his hair back with his fingers. "Naw. Come over here, kid. Or I'll come over there—I'm getting a little sloshed. You don't mind—it makes a pleasant change from your old man's orders, right? That may be one of the best things I've done in my life, getting your sister away from him. I always wondered—I *did*, you know, a lot, a lot for me anyway—how *you'd* do. How you'd hold up. To see if they'd get you. They get you, kid?"

"Naw," Bullet said, feeling the muscles across his shoulders.

"You were such a tough little bastard, I couldn't predict how things would turn out for you." Frank pushed his glass across the table and moved over to sit beside Bullet. "I got something to show you."

He pulled his wallet out of his back pocket and removed a picture. It was a photograph of a kid, a little kid. The kid was wearing just diapers and sitting on somebody's lap, but the grownup was mostly cut out of the picture, only her tanned arm showed, hugging the kid. The kid was tanned too, had a headful of dark baby hair, straight, and dark eyes looking right into the camera, serious. It was like the kid was looking right at Bullet and could see him.

"What is it?" Bullet asked.

"*It* is my kid," Frank told him. "More than a year ago. She'll be bigger now. What do you think?"

What am I supposed to think. What was Frank up to?

"And that's old Liza," Frank said.

Bullet turned his face to stare at Frank. The man was enjoying the joke.

"You're an uncle, kid. Whadda you think of that?"

Bullet didn't think anything.

"Maybe even twice by now. I don't know, I haven't heard anything from Liza for a year. She never was much at writing. And I've been out of touch. It's not easy to find a ship going to Boston these days. But she said, last letter that got to me, she thought she was pregnant again."

"Where is she?"

"Out on Cape Cod—unless she's moved. But Liza doesn't move, you know Liza. I got them a house, her and Dicey—that's the kid's name—a little rancher outside of town, three bedrooms, big picture windows for the view, wall-to-wall carpeting, the works. Her and Dicey and little whoever it turned out to be. I ought to go up and see them, don't you think?"

Bullet felt like his whole torso was squeezing in around his spine. He didn't know what to think. He wrapped his hand around the glass of ginger ale, half full and watery with melted ice. Frank was such a liar. He made such a point about the house, it had to be a lie. Bullet knew that, but he didn't know what the truth was. How bad it was. Stupid Liza, just like her, finding someone like Frank and having a kid. If he had her there he'd shake her, he'd shake some sense into her, shake her until her brains rattled—what there was of them. He wished . . . he wished he'd taken a flying tackle at her when she came running down the stairs that night to go off with Frank, he wished he'd brought her down and held her so she couldn't . . . He wished. Wishes were wishes and facts were facts. People did what they did, whether it was stupid or smart. Mostly it was stupid. And Bullet wasn't going to stupidly try to wish away what Liza had done, he wasn't going to let himself box himself in that way, wishing.

Frank just sat staring at the photograph, getting morose. "She's a good kid, spunky, you know? I never thought I'd like having a kid." Bullet looked at the photograph, too, and the muscles around his ribcage tightened.

He looked at Frank, who was just staring into the picture. Frank's mouth drooped down a little at the ends. "If I had the fare, I'd go up there right now, tonight; I could use a dose of Liza. She loves me—you know how she is—she really does love me, just me. I mean, I'm okay and all that, but I'm not such a great guy, you know?"

Yeah, Bullet agreed. He wanted to get out of there, but Frank blocked his way. He was about to bust Frank one in the face and he wanted to get out.

"I'm terrific, you know, but not much of a friend—sort of . . . Oh, hell, it doesn't matter. What's it matter, anyway—right, kid? The stupid cow loves me. It doesn't matter to her, whatever I do." He looked at Bullet without seeing him. "Or don't do. I got something to tell you, kid. You listening to me?"

Bullet's jaw ached, and the eyes suddenly focused on him.

"I wouldn't try it, kid. You don't last as long as I have without knowing how to take care of yourself. And you don't know anything, not anything. You hear me?"

Bullet heard, and he believed Frank, and he was angry—there was nothing he could do, there was never anything you could do, but he wanted to do something: he wanted to take Frank Verricker's teeth out.

"She won't marry me. Don't get me wrong, I don't much mind not being married. I told her I'd marry her, when she was pregnant. But not Liza. She even gave the kid her name, because I wasn't at the hospital to stop her. Tillerman, like I had nothing to do with it. She wouldn't have done that if I'd been there, I wouldn't have let her, you can believe me. It's not my fault—I told her I was willing. But not Liza. Just like her, too, stupid. If we were married they'd send her half my wages, more than half with a kid or two." At that he grinned again, and his voice got sentimental. "Old Liza," he said. "I wonder if . . . do you think Honey'd give me the money to get to Boston?"

Bullet shoved Frank out of his way and got out of the booth. *Just like Liza—stupid,* he thought, between waves of anger. He shoved his way out of the room, not caring who he plowed into.

Outside, it was growing dark. He stood in the crowded parking lot, trying to force air into his lungs. The cars were lined up, nose to nose. The long silver nose of Honey's car hung up over the cement curbing.

Bullet went around beside the roadhouse, seeing what there

was lying around on the ground, until he found himself a long, thick pipe. He came back with it to Honey's car. He lifted it back and swung it, down, onto the hood of the car. Metal rang on metal, echoing itself. He swung again, and again. The hood bent, dented, clanged—its smooth line got pocked. Breathing heavily from the effort—but it wasn't hard work, Bullet thought—he threw the pipe down on the ground.

Damn Frank Verricker.

He kicked at the front tire and strode out of the parking lot. At the road he turned toward town and ran. He ran tight and hard, his fists clenched as his arms swung up close to his chest.

It was after six when he got back. They were eating. They heard him come up the back porch, and his mother's eyes watched him enter the kitchen. His father did not look at him, but reached his fork out to the platter in front of him and speared another pork chop. His father wore a jacket and tie, his mother wore her fancy red blouse. Bullet stood by the sink in his jeans and T-shirt. At least he didn't have to change for dinner anymore.

He stared at the two of them. He had half a mind to tell them about Frank Verricker, he had half a mind to just sit down and grab a pork chop. And eat it with his fingers. What could the old man do, after all? Pick him up and tote him away from the table? The old man couldn't do anything to Bullet. As if Bullet wanted to sit down and eat with them.

They'd sit up and listen if I told them. I could tell them something that would make them sit up, if I felt like it.

The words burned their way up from his stomach. He took a breath, to start letting them out.

"Your father is wondering when those barn doors are going to be fixed," his mother said. Her eyes were fixed on his face, and they had no expression he could read.

His mouth clamped shut. *Right now.* Her head nodded at him, once, as if she had heard him. *Getting her to do his dirty work, always getting her to do it.*

Bullet went back outside. The evening light added to the light oozing out of the kitchen windows was enough to work by. He stood by the open barn doors, considering. He shoved with his shoulder against the one on the right. Either it would be fixed at the top, where the hinge hung askew, or it would be fixed at the bottom, where the wood bit into the uneven ground.

Bullet went into the barn, making his way into the darkness where the tools were kept. He felt around for the sledgehammer on the wall. Holding it over his shoulder, he went back to work on the doors.

The old wood gave way easily, with crackling sounds. He assumed they could hear the noise in the house, but nobody came out to watch him at work. Fixing the barn doors.

CHAPTER 13

Bullet hooked school the next day: he just got off the bus and went his own way. The thick, triple story of brick waited like a prison, and he didn't go in. Nobody could make him. They could, he guessed, capture him and drag him inside, if they could get a rope onto him—which he doubted.

Anyway, the question never arose. Hanging onto his lunch bag, he moved around the building and down to the playing fields. A couple of first-period gym classes were doing calisthenics, but he went on by them. Nobody asked him any questions. If anybody had, he wouldn't have answered, and if they'd come chasing after him he wouldn't have run. Nobody was going to make him run.

At the oval track he put down his lunch bag and stripped off his sweater and jeans. He folded them into a little pile, the bright red sweater on the brown earth. It was chilly, but the sun was already burning off the morning mist, and the day would grow warm. He ran the cross-country course, ran it five times, ran it hard. Nobody was going to stop him from running.

When the sweat on his chest had dried, he put on his shirt and tied the sweater around his waist by its arms. He walked along down into town, following the main street right up to where it ended at the water. Then he followed the water around to Patrice's, going through shallows when there was no public pathway. By the time he got out there, his sneakers were sodden and muddy and his jeans clung to his calves.

Patrice wasn't home. His truck was gone. Bullet went out and sat on the deck of *Fraternité* for a while. He would have hosed her down except she was always kept clean. He ate his sandwiches, then went back along the dock to drop the crumpled-up bag into Patrice's incinerator. He hung around the yard for a while, seeing what Patrice was up to. The fourteen-footer was almost finished. The ribs were in and boards ran its entire curved length—fitted so neatly you almost couldn't see that it was made of separate boards. A new transom lay nearby, needing sanding before it could be set into place, the joints cut out like pieces of a jigsaw puzzle. Bullet ran his hand along the sides of the boat, sanded to silky smoothness, ready for an undercoat. He didn't know how Patrice stood it, all that slow work, but he surely admired the results, and even admired Patrice for being able to achieve them.

He turned and looked around the yard. A couple of hulls, an empty boat trailer digging its nose into the ground, motors and propellers. Then he stepped over the picket fence.

The road by Patrice's was lined on both sides with little houses, each house surrounded by a yard and fence. The other yards, past which Bullet jogged, were planted and tended, kept neat. It bothered his neighbors that Patrice didn't plant and tend his lawn. Every now and then, somebody would write him a note, anonymous, of course, or a group of men would come to try to talk to him about keeping up the neighborhood. Patrice never minded them, but it made Bullet mad, and these little boxed-in gussied-up yards didn't show him anything either.

His return route took him through one of the colored sections. Not the higher income one, that was downtown. This was shacks along the roadside, built from tar paper over cinder-block footings; or old trailers with patches of vegetable gardens beside them; or once even an old bus, with a bedspread hung for a door. Bullet jogged past the section fast; it made him angry.

He arrived home by midafternoon and went right upstairs to get his gun. He stopped in the kitchen for a couple of glasses of milk, which he drank standing up, looking out the window over the sink. He could see his mother off around the corner, checking the sheets on the clothesline. They weren't dry yet, but a late-afternoon breeze was building up and that would probably finish the job. The cool milk flowed down his throat.

He heard heavy footsteps behind him, the old man. He didn't turn around, didn't hurry himself. He felt the old man's anger wash over him from behind and almost smiled. Slowly, he lifted the glass to empty it. Slowly, he turned on water, rinsed the glass, set it down slowly on the washboard. He wondered what the old man would do if he turned around to face him. He'd said he didn't want to lay eyes on Bullet. What would he do if Bullet turned around? . . . Run out of the room?

Bullet turned around.

His father was staring at the toes of his shoes and his eyes didn't even flicker, so Bullet knew the man had been staring at them all the time he'd been standing there. He could have laughed.

"There is nothing quite so childish as getting even by wanton destruction," the old man said to his shoes.

Bullet wondered what would happen if ten little voices answered back: "Yes, sir . . . yes, sir . . . yes, sir," overlapping one another like waves coming into shore. He stared at his father's bent head, to where the face began, under the white crown. He stared hard, wanting to force the guy to look up and eat his own words.

"You'll repair the damage you did."

I did what I was told. They close now—I checked that.

"They'll need to be completely rebuilt now."

So what?

"Then rehung. On new hinges." The orders came marching out. "You'll have to rebuild the frame first."

You can't make me.

"If not right away, you'll have to do it sooner or later, whenever—"

Bullet knew what he was about to get to. *Unh-uh, you're not going to do that to me.*

"When it's yours."

You can't make me.

"So that you have succeeded only in fouling your own nest. Like any other animal, like some nigger. I am not surprised at that, not surprised at all."

—not going to hang that around my neck. Box me in with it. Use it that way. Take it away from me. Because nothing felt under his feet the way the rich, flat acres of home did.

"Because the farm is yours, or as good as. Not that I particularly want to give it to you."

You don't want to give it to anyone, you want to pull it into your grave after you like some blanket.

"And I hope it chokes you like it's choked me."

Anger burned up in Bullet's guts and his bones closed in around it. He got his hands on his gun and got out of the room. His father wanted to make Bullet take it from him because he hated it; he couldn't make Bullet take anything from him. Nobody could do that, but nobody. They kept trying to box him in, and he kept breaking out—and he'd keep on breaking out, damn them.

He went around behind the barn and into a thin patch of woods. He moved fast, and his noisy progress routed two crows out of the branches. Without thinking, he shouldered, cocked, aimed the gun and fired twice. He got one. Not bad. Even with this second-rate gun, his marksmanship was okay, maybe even good. When he could pick up the Smith and Wesson in Salisbury, he'd be good enough for it.

Bullet slowed down, moving more quietly. In another couple of weeks the hunting season would begin, and he'd have to get himself a bright orange hat. But now he didn't have to worry about being picked off by some jerk from some city who mistook him for a deer, or maybe a duck. He thought, sliding the clip into place and shoving the bolt home, if he saw some ducks he might shoot for them. Game wardens stayed home as long as they could, earning their salaries by shuffling papers on a desk until they had to get out into the cold to actually keep an eye on things. It wasn't even cold yet, just crisp in the shady woods. If he flushed any ducks and was close enough, he might just shoot for them. Who'd see him here? Who could catch him?

All of his senses alert, he walked the woods and fields as the afternoon gathered in around him. Once he got a shot at a rabbit, off to the left inlaid, but he missed. He opened the bolt, picked up the empty casing and jammed it into his pocket, then slid the bolt home again, hearing the bullet click into place. For a while, he sat in a clearing, just in case a deer might come browsing by near enough to justify trying for it. Across the open space, the bare trees rose into a gray sky, each branch clear. A breeze flowed along the land, running for the water. It soughed through the pines, and the top-heavy loblollies swayed under its hands. No deer came by.

When Bullet moved back into the woods, it was twilight there, darker than in the open, the light dim and shadowy. He stopped, pulled his sweater over his head, and then—holding the twenty-two ready, like a pistol at his right hip—he tossed a couple of dead branches up into a pine, seeing if anything flushed out. Nothing moved.

But something moved off to his right, low and on the ground, at the edge of his vision. . . . He got the shot off before he even properly saw, a sweet reflex shot, his whole body coordinated and working like a perfect machine.

A good shot too, he heard the cry and the muffled thud of a small body falling to ground in mid-movement. His hands worked the bolt to reload the barrel automatically as he went over to the bushes to see what he'd gotten.

OD—the stupid mutt—lay on her side with blood coming out every time she breathed. Her eyes were closed.

Bullet knew what he had to do next. He raised the gun to his shoulder and aimed just behind her left eye. At this range, even this gun wouldn't fail him. "I *told* you," he said to her. He hooked his finger around the trigger. He wanted to do this in one clean shot. Why did she have to be so stupid?

At the sound of his voice she opened her eye and her tail wagged a couple of times. It barely rustled the leaves and branches she lay on.

"You stupid mutt," Bullet said. "What am I supposed to do?"

The tail moved again, and she tried to lift her head to see him, but apparently she couldn't.

Bullet crouched down beside her and took a look at the wound. It was a kind of ragged hole in her rib cage. She tried to turn, tried to get up—her front legs kind of scrabbled and her chest heaved; her back legs didn't move at all. Blood came out of the hole, slow and steady.

"What did you think you were doing?" he demanded. But she hadn't been thinking, and now look what had happened. She'd just been following him around and got in the wrong place at the wrong time. Stupid, just like Liza, and wagging her tail at him when he'd just pumped lead into her.

Bullet forced his rib cage outward with a breath.

Not his fault, he knew that.

His rib cage and the banded muscles of his diaphragm closed in again, putting pressure on his lungs.

She walked into it. Time and again, over and over, he'd sent her home. The stupid dog just wouldn't learn.

He forced breath into his lungs.

He felt like kicking her. It made him angry . . .. what she'd done.

His muscles bunched together and moved with anger. He rose, bent to pick up the twenty-two, stared down at the dog making a puddle of dark blood on the dried pine needles.

She lay there uncomplaining, breathing, bleeding—dying.

It wasn't his fault, but he had fired the shot. And now what was he supposed to do. He felt boxed in, helpless—caught in somebody else's trap, like always. He needed to yell, he needed to move, before the sides of the box pushed in all around him and crushed him.

He felt himself explode into action, swinging his arms—and he cracked the twenty-two against the twisted trunk of a swamp oak. The shock of the impact ran along his bones, jarring the shoulder socket and moving on, like a lightning bolt, down through the muscles of his back. He slammed it again and again. The noise he was making with his voice had no meaning, it just exploded out of him.

At last, the gun broke, snapped apart where the barrel joined the stock. The barrel flew off into the dark woods, landing with a crash. He threw the stock after it, listening to it fly through branches and crash down somewhere in the dark circle beyond visibility.

He was breathing heavily. He turned to look down at OD before walking away.

Her ears were up, listening. She didn't even know what was going on.

Bullet sat down on the rough ground by her head. "All right," he said aloud. "But hurry up." He put one hand on her head, rubbing a little with his fingers. He could feel the shape of her skull under the smooth hair. Her skull fit into his hand. If he wanted to, he could take his two hands and crush that circle of bone—if she'd been in pain he would have. His fingers moved behind her floppy ears. Along the edge of the delicate layer of bone.

She was small, OD, smaller even than that kid in the picture Frank showed him. Liza's kid. He didn't believe Liza had gone and had a kid, with Frank for the father—and maybe two. How stupid could anyone be.

You're not looking too smart to me right now, he told himself.

It wasn't my fault, he answered.

Yeah, but it's your responsibility.

Well, I'm accepting that, so shut up.

He shut up.

OD breathed slowly, patiently, waiting. Bullet breathed beside her, waiting. Night settled slowly in around them, sifting in among the trees. She wasn't complaining, OD. She wasn't scared. Little night noises moved around them, scurryings and flutterings, the rustling of leaves and sometimes a distant motor, some boat moving back to harbor.

Bullet felt the hard ground under his backside and his legs. His shoulders rested back against a fallen tree. His one hand rested on OD's skull, the little finger going down along her neck to register the shallow rise and fall of her breathing.

He sat between anger and sad. They felt the same, the sad and the anger. He could see the shapes of trees and the massy shape of undergrowth, but nothing more. He could see, turning his head slightly, the whitish shape of OD.

"I'm sorry, OD," he finally spoke aloud. He barely recognized his own voice. He heard a rustle of dried pine needles where her tail was. "I dunno, I wish you hadn't walked into it. I wish I hadn't taken that shot—I didn't mean to."

If she knew anything, which he doubted, she'd know that was true. Which didn't make any difference. "You're such a stupid mutt, OD," his voice said, trying to tell her, "but you've been okay." And she couldn't possibly understand, he knew that. "You've been an okay dog, all things considered."

Shut up, he told himself.

Well, she was.

Night folded in over them. The wind picked up, and he could no longer hear OD's breathing. He could only feel it through his fingers. The moon must have risen, because the woods were infiltrated with silver clouds of light that made patches of dark shadows. The shadows moved, where they ran through trees. The wind washed cold over Bullet. He didn't move. He stayed and waited. He had no idea how much time passed and he didn't care. And then, quietly, OD was no longer breathing. Because he had killed her.

He got up, stiff and angry. But he was angry at himself. He didn't know what to do about that.

Johnny was right, you're a breaker, he told himself. *She had courage. She was nothing but a stupid mutt, and she did it right. Good for you, OD.*

CHAPTER 14

In the shadowy woods, there wasn't anything he could dig a grave with. He started digging with his fingers where he'd been sitting, but after the layer of dead needles and dried leaves scraped off, and the top dusty layer of soil, all he could do was scratch uselessly. He felt around until he found a stick, strong enough. He used that to scrape and pry and dig into the soil. With his hands, he scooped out the handfuls of soil he loosened that way and piled it by his knees. Then he scraped and pried again.

After a long time, he had made a shallow grave. He picked up the body of the dog—just a body now, empty—and put her into it. Scraping with his hands, he covered her over with dirt. After the dirt, he piled on armloads of leaves, and finally, with the heaviest branches he could find, he made a covering. He set the branches side by side in a straight row over the grave.

He stood up, cold and stiff, but not tired. *That was such a stupid thing to do. A stupid mistake. Mine.*

Bullet made his way down to the water and went north toward the farm. Along by the water the sky showed stars and moon overhead. Liza should have taken OD with her. Liza knew what it was like. Leaving OD there was like— Bullet splashed up through the cold shallows. It was like lions, the way the old man—and he did it too—devoured things. Like lions attacking and chasing down, teeth and claws and the powerful relentless bodies. Then ripping her apart, ripping the flesh and bones apart, and the blood, guts, everything lying on the ground. . . . Poor OD didn't have a chance, nobody could have stopped them.

Come off it, he said to himself. *What kind of an idea is that?*

It's just an idea, he answered, *but it's my own, and maybe even the first one all my own. So get lost.*

Get lost (scornfully), *how can I get lost? Jerk.*

Bullet agreed.

He turned at the dock, to go inland. Over the marsh grasses the sky lightened to silver, and a streak of orangy pink heralded the sunrise. Bullet stopped to watch. He wasn't in any hurry.

As the light rose above a line of trees, it flowed like water over the grasses, turning them warm brown, almost gold. They swayed, as if the light were a hand passing over them. The distant trees assumed color.

Bullet headed up the path. He came through the pines into his mother's vegetable garden. There the brown harrowed earth shone under early sunlight, and the few dark leaves hanging on the tomato plants glowed. A couple of pumpkins were hidden away under broad flat leaves, their vines twisting along the rough earth. Tiny tentacles went out from the vines to hold the soil. He bent down and took a handful of dirt, rubbing it with his fingers against his palm, letting it shower down. You grew things out of this, and his fingers could feel its richness.

He looked toward the house and met his mother's eyes. She was sitting on the back steps, still in the clothes she'd worn for dinner, red shoes with heels, blue skirt, the white blouse. He walked toward her. Her hands held a blanket around her shoulders. Her eyes were fixed on his face. She had been waiting for him.

"Maw," he said.

She didn't answer. Her face stayed expressionless.

"What are you *doing*?" he demanded.

"You took your gun," she snapped.

He turned, looked where she was looking, over the garden to the marsh. He sat down beside her, so his shoulder almost touched hers. He could feel how she was feeling, and he didn't like feeling that; he didn't like her feeling it either; it made him angry that she should have to.

With his shoulder touching hers, he tried to tell her. "I shot OD." He waited, and she didn't say anything. "It was an accident. Anyway, I waited with her—and then I had to bury her."

The two of them sat looking out. He waited for what she would answer. He wouldn't blame her if she let fly at him.

"People like us," she finally said, "I dunno, boy. Innocent, weak things come into our hands, and we do such a bad job by them. We destroy them."

"It wasn't like that; it was an accident," he told her.

She turned her head to face him, her eyes burning. "Don't pretend, boy. Are you pretending to yourself you didn't do it? Because if you are, you're lying to yourself. Are you doing that? Are you going to do that to yourself?"

Her anger drove the breath out of him, and he pulled his body back from hers. "But," he started to say, and her mouth moved without saying anything. She wasn't talking to him, he understood that; he understood her anger.

"No, I'm not," he promised her. Her head nodded once, sharply. *What a life for her,* he suddenly thought, angry and sad again. *Why didn't she get out, why doesn't she?*

"You don't know," she said.

"No, I don't think I do," he told her. Then a sudden question drove everything else out of his head.

"Do you think I should have carried her home? Do you think a vet could have done anything? Momma?"

She asked him to describe the wound, so he did, his answers as quiet as her questions. He didn't try to explain how it happened, just talked about what OD looked like. His mother thought about it, then shook her head. "No, bringing her home wouldn't have been any good."

Bullet believed her, but he couldn't be sure.

"Besides, we'd have had to sail into town to find a vet," his mother said.

"And I wouldn't have liked to bury her in the water," Bullet said.

"Agreed."

They sat in silence. Bullet was cold, he realized. "You should go inside," he said.

"I am tired, I am that." But she didn't get up. "And my feet hurt."

"Take off your shoes. Why didn't you take off your shoes?"

"And ruin a pair of perfectly good stockings?"

"Take off your stockings too."

"Bare feet are common," she reminded him.

"You don't think that," he told her. *Talk about boxes.*

She didn't answer. He guessed he knew why.

"Maw?" he said. "You're the stubbornest old woman in the world."

A smile moved across her face and was gone. Watching that, Bullet thought: *How long has it been? What a life for her,* and then, loud inside his own head, *I won't let him do this to her.*

And what are you going to do? he asked himself. *What can you do?*

Something.

You're the breaker. You destroy. You forgotten already?

No. No, I haven't.

He thought maybe he could tell her about Frank's visit, just about the picture of the kid. But then he recognized that that wouldn't be much joy to her, finding out she had a grandchild, and maybe two, that she didn't even know where they were and wouldn't be able to get off the farm to go find them even if she wanted to. That would just be adding more boards to the side of her box, making her box squeeze tighter on her. It would be like turning her into prey, sticking his lion's claws and teeth into her. He couldn't get her out of her box any more than he could unshoot the shot that got OD. There was nothing he could do.

Everybody was in the same box, helpless. She was and he was—and maybe even the old man, although Bullet couldn't see that, but maybe she could—and everybody. *What a world.*

"I don't recall any orders about me cooking for you, do you?" Bullet asked his mother. He stood up. She looked at him.

"You used to have a sense of humor," she told him. Her hair, streaked with gray, hung in a braid down her back.

Bullet couldn't make any sense out of that remark. He wondered if he'd been wrong about her, overestimated her strength.

"A good one," she said, thoughtfully.

"I still do," Bullet told her and wondered if she was cracking up, had been cracking, slowly, over the years, while they—him and the old man—lionlike, devoured her.

She snorted. "You could fool me."

Then Bullet saw what she meant and did smile. "I doubt that—I never could fool you. I've got eggs and some bacon. I fry me a mean egg. We could eat standing up." He wanted to give her something, even just breakfast.

She shook her head. "No. No I can't do that."

Anger rose up in Bullet again, and again sad. "Stubborn," he told her, "stubborn *and* proud. I dunno, Maw, you're gonna get yourself into trouble."

That brought another smile to her face, a sudden smile, as suddenly gone. She knew what he was thinking. "You, boy," she said.

He left her there on the back steps, with her face turned to the garden, the marsh, and if she could have seen beyond it, the water.

CHAPTER 15

Bullet dozed his way through that morning's classes. He would enter a classroom as the bell rang, slouch down in his seat with his legs stretched out, let his chin fall down onto his chest and close his eyes. Images played against the dark screen of his lowered eyelids, and voices sounded inside his head, all the pictures and sounds jumbled together. He couldn't keep track of them. He felt off balance, as if his muscles were running without any central controlling agency, and he would sense outward to where his ankles crossed, or his arms folded across his stomach, to reassure himself of his own stillness. Then he would doze off. Next thing he knew, the bell rang and he got up to go to his next class.

He ate lunch outside, feeling pretty rested, considering, as he leaned back against the bricks and chewed at his sandwiches. A chilly wind blew against his face and the sun shone sharp. He wouldn't be able to sleep during shop. They didn't even have chairs, just tall stools. So he turned away from the lines of moving students, drifted around the back of the building and headed for the street. Once there, he started to run. He ran fast, hard, the three miles to Patrice's. Whatever else, his body was in good working order, working well to his orders.

Patrice opened the door, surprised to see him, the dark eyes sharp and curious, although all he said was, "Come in." He had covered his table with newspapers and spread the parts of a motor on that. He was cleaning the parts, with gasoline in a plastic basin. "You have come early."

Bullet peeled off his sweater and sat down. Patrice got back to work, his hands scrubbing, polishing. "When I think of it, you are the opposite of that dillar-a-dollar scholar—you come a little earlier now. You aren't racing with your team," he added. Bullet looked up. "I deduce this from your name not being mentioned in the newspaper." He reached out a hand and dripped gasoline onto an article in front of Bullet. "The sports section."

"I didn't know you read the paper."

"It is only once a week; they send it to me for nothing. Sometimes, when I spread it out, my eye glances over it."

"You're laughing at me."

"Yes, a little. Do you mind?"

Bullet shrugged.

"If you want to do something, you could clean these spark plugs. Not that lazy scraping with a screwdriver, but with this steel wool. Do you want to do that?"

"Okay. But I wondered, there are a few hours, we could go out for some oysters."

Patrice shook his head. Bullet got up and stood looking out a window toward the dock. "I have emptied the gas tank, there is a leak. . . ." Behind him, Patrice's voice went on, describing how he would solder the cracked metal. Bullet let the words flow around him, not listening. He would have liked a few hours of hard labor.

"Hello, hello," Patrice said. Bullet turned around. "It isn't that you need the money, is it?"

Bullet shook his head. "I just thought," he said. He sat down again and picked up a piece of steel wool. "Is this for the fourteen-footer?" he asked.

"No, for that one I'll get a new motor, I've decided that. Nothing but the best. It will be my best work, that one."

They worked in silence for a long time. Bullet stared at his own hands, working patiently, slowly. He concentrated on his fingers, scouring at the crud and chemical deposits on the spark plugs. Patrice soaked, scrubbed and polished dry, not talking for a change. Bullet's legs and shoulders wanted to move, wanted to work, but he concentrated on his fingers. Finally, Patrice asked, "Something is wrong?"

Bullet met the bright dark eyes and said nothing, did nothing, didn't even shrug. His mind seemed frozen, caught in some kind of panic, like a cramped muscle. Patrice waited and Bullet answered him at last. "Yeah. Something I did, I don't like it. What I did."

"This is a phenomenon?"

"Yeah. I know how that sounds, but it's true. Always before I liked what I did." He smiled reluctantly. "I know it's funny."

"I don't know about funny, but lucky."

Bullet did laugh then. *Lucky.*

Patrice saw the humor, but protested: "I mean it. There comes a time when you can no longer compromise. I've amused you again, but I mean that. I could be wrong, but I do mean it." He got up from the table. "If you will put these things away, please, and clear up the mess, I'll begin dinner. You'll stay?"

"Sure." *Compromise?* Well, maybe.

Carefully, Bullet took up the parts of the dismantled outboard, setting them down on fresh newspapers spread out on a shelf. He gathered up the soiled papers from the table and shoved them into the wastebasket. He washed his hands, to get the gas off them.

Patrice took a chicken out of the refrigerator and set it on the counter, where he disjointed it with a cleaver. Bullet didn't want to talk about OD, but there was something he did want to know: "How'd you know?" he asked Patrice's back.

The shoulders shrugged beneath a plaid woollen shirt. "You

have the appearance of having slept in your clothes. You have stubble on your head. You usually take care of your appearance; not because you are vain, I think, but proud."

Bullet ran his hand over his scalp, then over his chin. The scant hairs on his face were soft, but his head felt rough, scratchy. "I forgot."

"Which is not like you," Patrice said.

Bullet didn't say anything.

Patrice dried the pieces of chicken with a paper towel. Then he took out mustard, oil and a head of garlic, from which he pulled off two cloves. He crushed those, then mixed all the ingredients together in a small bowl. He melted butter on the stove, brushed that over the chicken pieces and set them under the broiler. He started some rice, cut two tomatoes in half and put them on a baking sheet, then sat down to shell some peas. Bullet stood watching, waiting for Patrice to speak. It was obvious that there was something Patrice was going to say.

"When I was fifteen, and the Germans came," his light voice said as his fingers clumsily pulled apart the pods, "I had no family in our village. The couple who had raised me—they had a dairy herd and a small business for making cheese, they needed a boy for the labor. When the Germans came, they had fled the village. I was nothing to them, just a boy for the labor. So I became a messenger for the Macquis—the Resistance? You've heard of it?"

Bullet had. He sat down across from Patrice. When his mother shelled peas, it was with one hand, holding the long pods at her fingertips, then squeezing until they split open to let the green pellets fall into the bowl. Patrice, missing fingers, needed both hands.

"I was small and clever. I knew the countryside. I was a courier, a runner. I had my message memorized; we never used anything written down. I was too young, too—weak, physically, to be used in raids or as escort to travelers. They called me L'ancien, the old one. So you see, I even had my own code name. And I was proud.

"When I was brought in for questioning—

"You see, we had destroyed a bridge, a railroad bridge that spanned a broad ravine, a supply route. Our work was to plan and achieve such destruction, to impede and hinder whenever possible. After a success, of course, the enemy reacted strongly. As we had known they would.

"You see, we were a country town, a farming town, unimportant, except for their pride. So when I was brought in—

"What I had to conceal was a route along which we could move people, our own or those who were escaping from the country into the mountains, into Spain. The enemy knew—because we also had our traitors—that there was a party of men traveling at that time. They did not know where, or when. That, I knew. Why their choice fell on me, I don't know—except that perhaps they realized at last that a boy with no ties, no family upon whom retribution might fall, was a boy the Macquis might use."

Patrice looked straight at Bullet, who sat listening. "They were correct. And very angry. They had been made to look foolish—a Resistance cell operating under the very noses, under the very moustaches. The interview did not take long, and much of it I do not remember. Memory selects—I do not recall the fear, or the pain—which is not surprising. Those are physical sensations. They are either to come, present, or past. When present they dominate. Before, after—they *are* not. That is curious, isn't it?"

Bullet wasn't interested in the speculative question. "What—?"

"If I work for it, I can bring up the sound of the voices, questioning. Even after all these years. I can see the cleaver—an ordinary kitchen cleaver very like my own—with which they threatened me, and my hands I can see, spread out onto the sheet that covered the tabletop. Because the blood shoots out so."

Patrice looked down at his hands. Bullet had his eyes on Patrice's gnome face.

"Courage I have. Of vanity . . ." He shrugged, and his eyes were humorous. ". . . little. They questioned. I continued my pretense of ignorance, and the terror was no pretense. I remember it, as if it were not my own event, as if I had not been there, myself. The boy at the table and the men around him. Then, I hear a voice behind me, some officer who has just come into the interrogation room, and he asks, *Who is this boy?* and then my courage failed. They could know by asking, and nobody had been interested—just another boy, orphaned and ordinary, a scrawny and uncared for boy who survived somehow. But we knew by then the workings of their minds, and what they did to such as I."

"What do you mean such as you?" Bullet wondered, but Patrice went on.

"So I told them—how large a party, from what direction, along which route, at what time. Even then, I hoped to warn the party. That was what I hoped, to make meaningless my betrayal. I knew the countryside, I was quick enough, the information would be useless to them. They were pleased. They pulled a brand from the fire—it was October then, too, and cold, as it is in October in my own country, frosts there begin in September. They cauterized the wounds—an act of mercy perhaps. I fainted.

"You see, I had not known I would faint. You can understand that. I had not known I would lose those minutes—how many were lost I do not know, except that they had carried me outside and left me. For anyone who passed by to see, and take warning. So that when I arrived at the place I had told them of, a long passage between hills, a narrow pathway, which I approached from a ridge . . .

"I was too late. The party—too distant to call out—they moved like shadows among trees, among rocks. The enemy lay in wait, concealed along the hillside, silent. The party had some arms, rifles, pistols, knives of course. They moved like herded sheep into the ambush.

"While I watched.

"I had to stay to make the report. Six men, twenty soldiers—the soldiers moved to encircle the party before they made their attack. They wanted captives, of course. This the men knew.

"All of the soldiers commenced firing at a signal, to wound and disable. We were accustomed to act quickly and take what shelter afforded. For a few minutes, the air was filled with gunshots. I watched and counted. The enemy closed its circle. When only two of the party were left alive—there is a stillness to the dead that is unmistakable, and a man whose brains lie outside of his skull will not live—the enemy ceased firing. The soldiers stood to rush. One man was on the ground, helpless; the other stood against a tree because his leg ran with blood. He had some time, he had some ammunition. He shot his wounded companion, then fired into the rush of soldiers, who automatically fired back as their captain called out orders to stop them.

"Of the twenty, eight returned unharmed, and they bore with them five wounded. Of the six, none."

Patrice's hands went back to work. Bullet waited for the point of the story.

"This I reported, that same night, because it had to be known what information the enemy had. This I reported weeping with shame and regret. 'Don't be a fool,' they told me. 'Your body betrayed you—you did not betray us.' They sent me away, to the coast."

Patrice dumped the pods into the garbage. He turned the pieces of chicken in the broiler. He ran a pot of water for the peas, putting a spoonful of sugar into it. He stirred the mustard mixture and took a jar of bread crumbs out of the refrigerator.

"Why tell me about it?" Bullet asked. "I don't get it."

Patrice answered without turning around. "I have told only two people, who needed to know if I was equal to an assignment. They both felt—pity, mercy, compassion—although that was not their main concern, nor why I told them. After many years I tell it again. And you, you are pitiless."

That was true enough. "What good does pity do?"

"I don't criticize. I didn't tell you for the pity of it. I only observe." He pulled the pan of chicken out of the broiler and proceeded to paint it with the mustard coating, then cover each piece with bread crumbs and dribble butter over that. "Chicken diablo," he announced, slipping it back into the broiler. "After the years of hunger, I never tire of food."

"Patrice, I really don't understand," Bullet said.

"Ah. Will you set the table? I didn't know if you knew you didn't understand. It's good to know that."

"You aren't making any sense," Bullet said. He got up and set the table, knives, forks, napkins, glasses. He wanted to know what the story was supposed to mean, because he had a feeling it meant something, and Patrice thought it would mean something to him.

"Because my body betrayed me, but I think your spirit betrays you, and you can no longer compromise that. I should have warned you, it is speculative thought."

Well, Bullet was willing to consider that. "I didn't think compromising was what I did," he said.

"As if you had no heart," Patrice told him.

"Look, Patrice," Bullet warned the man. Patrice's face was not afraid, just concerned; the eyes steady and the full mouth still. Bullet felt his shoulders sag. He couldn't work out the connections, but he could feel them. He poured himself a glass of milk and set the carafe of white wine by Patrice's place. Because he could see that he might have been betraying himself—and Patrice was right, the provocation was no excuse. "Can I use your phone?" he asked.

He dialed, and waited through the long ringing: The phone was on his father's desk. Finally, his mother picked it up. "It's me," he said. "I'm calling to say I won't be home until later."

"Bullet?" she asked.

"Yeah. I'm having dinner in town."

She waited a few seconds. "That has nothing to do with me," she said.

"I *know* that," he answered, irritated.

"Just so you do," she snapped.

Then Bullet grinned into the phone. He knew what it was. The old man was right there listening, and she was making it clear to him, and to Bullet, where she stood. "Are we alone?" he whispered loudly into the phone.

She didn't know what to say, he could hear that. He waited. He could almost hear her thinking.

"You," she said.

"Me," he agreed. They hung up.

CHAPTER 16

Patrice set two plates on the table: pieces of chicken, a mound of white rice with the butter yellowing it, the bright red tomato halves baked until they were just browned on top and the little green peas. The chicken tasted crisp with bread crumbs, tangy with mustard, sweet with meat. "Good," Bullet said.

"Superb," Patrice corrected him.

They ate without speaking for a few minutes. Then Bullet said, "You were a guerilla. I didn't know they had guerillas back then."

"Oh, the American education," Patrice cried dramatically, without breaking the rhythm of his knife and fork. It was one of his favorite themes, how much Bullet hadn't learned. "You have such ignorance."

"I wasn't even alive then. How am I supposed to know?"

"It is history, history and common sense. Perhaps you might not know history, but you should expect of yourself common sense. What does the Bible say? There is nothing new under the sun."

"So what?"

"So you should know that guerilla warfare is as old as man. It is the method of the weaker side against the stronger. The Israelites used it to take Canaan, small bands of fighters, striking swiftly at a single objective, then withdrawing. Armies," Patrice theorized, "are a modern development."

Bullet thought about that. "Un-unh," he said. "That won't hold. Alexander the Great used an army, with elephants, I remember that."

Patrice agreed with him.

"And that Persian you told me about, with his ten thousand deathless soldiers."

"The *anthanatoi*, yes. Well, you are correct. So tell me, my friend, why you are no longer running."

"I am running."

"You are so precise. Let me rephrase it: Will you tell me why you are no longer running in the school races?"

"It doesn't matter."

"It is a change. And I think it does matter to you because you do it well. To me also, because I liked to think of you doing excellently well. And to read about you in the paper, which they send me free in the mail."

"The coach wanted me to train one of the other runners," Bullet explained. "I told him I wouldn't. He threw me off the team. That's all," Bullet said. "I'm still running."

"Do you mind this?"

"Not really." Bullet ate steadily.

"Curious," Patrice said. "Why didn't you want to work with this other boy? You wouldn't fear the competition, that I know. Did you think you weren't an adequate trainer?"

"I never thought about that side of it. No, the guy is colored is all. I probably could show him some stuff."

Patrice looked across the table at him, surprised. "Colored?"

Bullet shrugged. He guessed they'd just never talked about coloreds, he and Patrice. The question never came up between them, and why should it? "I don't mix with them, that's all."

Patrice's face, his eyes especially, looked amused.

"What's so funny about that?" Bullet demanded.

Patrice bent his face to study his plate, hiding his expression. He cut the last of his chicken off the bone but did not lift his fork. "Your coach, what did he say to that?"

"Just what you'd expect—about the team and winning."

"Ah. He wouldn't know how little you think of those."

"Nope," Bullet agreed, getting back to his food. He was looking forward to his second helpings. Patrice's shoulders were shaking. "What is so damned funny?"

"I am, myself, *colored*, as you call it." Patrice looked up, laughing.

"That's not funny." Sometimes Patrice's sense of humor irked him. "That's not what I meant."

"But I am. Well, in part. In an eighth part—"

No.

"—an octaroon. What is the phrase for it? A nigger in my woodpile?"

Bullet got up and walked out of the room. He strode across the dirt yard and jumped the fence. Angry, so angry he couldn't contain it all in his body. Patrice . . . colored.

He stopped at a loblolly and slammed his fist into it.

But Patrice was just . . . French?

No.

Stupid. Blind.

He turned around and looked back at the little house. *He liked Patrice.*

He didn't know what to do. He didn't even, he recognized with helpless fury, know what he wanted to do.

Bullet walked back over the fence and across the yard. He stood in the doorway, not entering the room. Patrice had gotten up to serve himself a couple of pieces of chicken, a wing and a thigh, with some rice and tomato. He turned around at the sound of the screen door slamming into place.

"I assumed that you knew."

"How could I know?"

"As everybody else does." At least he wasn't laughing now. He seemed to have figured out that it was serious, and he looked solemn, solemn and sad. "By my features, my hair, my pigmentation."

"Pigmentation?" Bullet demanded.

"Skin color."

"I thought you were just tan, you know that."

"No, I don't know that. I am tanned, too, as well."

"You lied to me."

"No, my friend, I didn't do that."

Bullet left the room, the house. He got as far as the fourteen-footer, where he sat down. He leaned his back against the curved wooden side. *Aw, Patrice.*

He leaned his elbows on his knees and locked his fingers behind his neck. Night fell over his shoulders. He stared into the impenetrable earth, calling himself names.

When he looked up, he saw the little house, painted bright white and set back from the water, in the fashion of watermen's houses. The square, uncurtained windows shone yellow. He saw Patrice, sitting at the table, not eating.

He knew Patrice, he'd worked with him, eaten with him, he respected him. Well, he did. He liked him. It wasn't as if he even liked that many people. His mother, underneath it all, yes. Tommy he used to. *And Patrice.*

About himself, Bullet knew that he could make his choices and pay the price. But this time—he guessed it was what Patrice had called his heart—whatever it was, it was rising up against him, refusing to compromise this time. Not willing to lie.

Yeah, but—

But, what, stupid. You didn't know; there's a lot you don't know.

A lot I do, too.

Okay, I'll give you that, but a lot to learn.

I've been looking at things wrong?

Find out.

Yeah, but—

Bullet got up and went back inside again. He sat down in his chair, at the table, his fists in his lap.

Patrice's face was almost comical in its seriousness. "I am sorry. If I had ever considered it, I would have thought. Perhaps—although perhaps not."

"I don't understand—" Bullet mumbled.

"My mother's grandmother, from Martinique, was a mulatto—half black, half white. It was all written down, in the records of the province, it was no secret, there was no shame. It was not my negro blood which marked me as a child, but illegitimacy. I knew my mother's name, but she had emigrated after my birth, and her family wanted nothing to do with me; I was shame to them. I knew all this, the French have a passion for records. This was why I was given to the childless couple in another village. The shame came from my birth, not my blood."

"What does illegitimate matter?" Bullet demanded.

Patrice shrugged. "There, it did. Every people has its own prejudices. When the Germans came, then my blood mattered. Had they looked, the records were all there. And to be sent to a camp—I could not have withstood that, I think. Had I thought about it, about you, I would not have thought you felt like that. You see? I would not have thought you were like that."

Bullet looked at the man. "What would you have thought I was like?"

Patrice's face creased into a smile, but not from laughter. "That is easy, because it struck me even when I first met you and you were still a boy. You were even then like some few men I had known, two men, both dead. Strong and hard—in your spirit—pitiless and ruthless, that too. Alone. They were men of bronze. I thought, when I first met you, that it was curious to meet such a man when he was a boy. In a different time of history—do you know? You captured my imagination, to see how you would grow."

Because Patrice understood him.

"I never intended to cause you pain," Patrice said.

I know. "It's not," Bullet said. "I know that," he said.

They sat for a long time, silent. Finally, Patrice said, "I don't have a dessert ready, but I can offer you seconds." He picked up his fork and knife and started to eat again.

Bullet knew that if he picked up his plate, got another piece of chicken and sat down to eat it, he was making promises. Promises he would keep, because he kept promises, like his mother, like Liza. Promises to take Patrice as he was, with the colored thrown in. But the colored had been thrown in long before he knew. The colored had always been thrown in—only Bullet didn't even know that until now. Patrice was what Patrice was. Once you got past the colored—which was where Bullet had always been, up until just that night—Patrice was just himself. Just the man he was. Which was all Bullet was, too, or all anyone was. The only thing that mattered was the kind of man you were.

Bullet stood up. Patrice didn't look at him, but his hands stopped moving.

"How is that chicken cold?" Bullet asked. He picked up his plate and went to the pan on the counter.

"It is as good cold as it is hot, I promise you," Patrice said. He turned around in his chair to watch Bullet.

"That's okay by me then," Bullet told him, "because it was pretty good hot."

The next day, Bullet stood by the door to the cafeteria, leaning against the wall, watching. People moved past him, leaving the lunchroom, occasionally glancing sideways at him and then away. He waited.

When Tamer came by, Bullet called to him. “Shipp.”

Tamer halted, wary. His friends moved on a little way, standing by. “Yeah,” he said.

“Do you want to do some work?”

The heavy eyebrows raised, questioning.

“Running,” Bullet said.

“What, with you?”

Bullet nodded. Tamer dismissed his friends with a glance, and they moved off into the throng. He studied Bullet, who studied him right back.

“What is it, you miss the glory?”

“No,” Bullet told him.

“Don’t you have *any* sense of humor?” Tamer demanded.

“Yes,” Bullet told him.

Tamer chuckled. “You could have fooled me, Whitey.” Bullet didn’t say anything. “What did the coach say?” Tamer asked. They stood four feet apart, and the crowd gave them room.

“I haven’t said anything to him,” Bullet answered. “He’ll say that he knew I had team spirit. That I had him worried. That my heart is in the right place.”

“It isn’t, though, is it,” Tamer said.

Bullet shrugged.

“Then what are you up to?” Tamer asked.

“Nothing,” Bullet said. “Do you want to do some work? Or not.”

Tamer thought. “It can’t do any harm. Okay, Tillerman, you’re on.” He moved away.

Bullet went to class.

They didn’t approach the coach together, but Tamer was there when Bullet trotted up at the start of practice. The coach came to greet Bullet and shook his hand. "I knew it," he said happily. "I knew you had some team spirit, kid. It's good to see you." He clapped Bullet on the shoulder.

Bullet didn't say anything.

"You had me worried, I'll tell you."

Bullet flicked a glance toward Tamer's face. The guy was trying not to smile.

"But your heart is in the right place, just like I thought."

Tamer coughed into his hand.

"So. You two guys made up a schedule or anything?" the coach asked.

"No," Bullet said. Tamer was still choking away in the background.

"I'll leave it up to you, kid. We're gonna have ourselves one hellava team. One sweet hell of a team," he repeated. "All right, let's get going," he called. "You okay, Shipp? You got a cold or something?"

CHAPTER 17

Okay," Tamer said. He and Bullet stood warily together, facing one another. Practice was over and everybody else had gone back, to cars and buses; the sun was lowering, the air growing sharp. "What do I have to do? Don't expect me to enthuse, Tillerman."

Bullet wasn't expecting anything. "There's speed and there's stamina," he said. He looked at the big colored guy: "What are you, six two? Weight one ninety?"

"One seventy."

He had a dark shadow, too, over his jawbone and above his lip. He looked full grown.

"Twenty in the spring," Tamer said, bored. "Blood type O-positive. C'mon, Tillerman, let's hear it, I've got other things to do."

"Nobody's making you," Bullet said.

"We going to work out or not?" Tamer insisted.

"Stamina first. I usually run ten miles."

"Ten?"

Bullet nodded.

"Every day?"

Bullet nodded.

"No wonder you outclass us."

Don't kid yourself, it isn't just the practice time.

"You would anyway, though, wouldn't you."

Bullet knew when he was being baited.

"So these races are diddly squat to you."

Bullet just went on with the business at hand. "You want to be able to run seven or eight, but you've got to work up to that."

"It's already the second week in October, I don't have much time. I've run four miles."

"Once. And barely," Bullet reminded him.

"Every day since then," Tamer answered. "I don't get caught in the same trap twice, Whitey. What's the longest these courses get, at our level?"

"Five miles and that's only the championship course."

"So I'm looking for six, six easy. Correct?"

Bullet shrugged. He was looking for seven or eight, but if he wanted to know better and shave it down to six, if he needed to feel like he was making all the decisions himself, that was no skin off Bullet's nose.

Tamer continued: "So I should do this course, once more around."

"It's no good unless you do six consecutively."

"Yeah, well, I can see that, but I can also see the sun getting lower. Let's get this over with."

Tamer chugged steadily along the cross-country path. Bullet kept back just behind him, feeling like he was barely moving at all. About halfway around the course, the colored guy fagged out—he leaned even further forward, his arms hung at his side, his feet just barely got off the ground. Dogged, he stumbled through the last mile. Then he collapsed full length onto the grass.

Bullet waited for him to catch his breath.

"What a way to make your name in athletics," Tamer groaned, rolling over and sitting up.

"You're big for a runner," Bullet pointed out.

"You're not exactly small," Tamer answered. "I was going to go out for football, but—" He looked back to the course he had run. "I never saw you running this five times. How do you get in ten miles?"

"I've got a course I run, at home."

Tamer stood up. Sweat ran down his cheeks and stained his gray T-shirt. "I'll run that with you."

Bullet shook his head. "Nothing personal."

Tamer looked at him without pleasure.

"My old man would probably take a shot at you. He won't have coloreds on the place."

"Blacks," Tamer said.

"Nothing personal," Bullet said. "We could do the job quicker and better there. But he's a crack shot."

"You aren't kidding," Tamer said.

Bullet didn't answer. Of course he wasn't kidding.

"Like father like son, huh? Just a chip off the old block, the old white block. Save your breath, Tillerman, I don't need to hear it." He got up. "Okay. I'll do this one again. You can go home, Tillerman, you've made your point. I'll make it around fine without your company. Better without."

"Fine by me, Shipp." Bullet turned around and jogged back toward the school. Behind him he heard the heavy feet start off again.

After a couple of days, the colored guy didn't start fading out until just after the fifth mile. Tamer ran the cross-country route three consecutive times, every day, staying for an hour after practice let out. Bullet hung around and ran the third lap behind him. He could almost predict where the big legs would start to run sloppy. On the third day of this, when Tamer collapsed at the finish, Bullet told him, "You've got to run through it."

"Shut up, Whitey." Tamer lay stretched out on his back, his big chest heaving.

"Suit yourself." Bullet started off. Suiting himself.

"Hey!" The colored guy yelled after him.

Bullet turned around. *Now what?* Tamer was sitting up, his legs out, rubbing his calves.

"Where are you going?"

"Look, Shipp, if you don't want to do this, it's fine by me."

"I don't want to, but I'm going to," Tamer said. "I figured you felt the same way."

Bullet could have grinned, it was so exactly what he was thinking. "So?"

"Whaddaya mean *so?* I thought you were supposed to be coaching me, not just proving your superiority. You don't know shit about coaching, Tillerman."

Bullet didn't argue.

"You know what I'm beginning to think? I'm beginning to think you think I don't know a mug's game when I see one."

"Apparently you don't," Bullet told him.

Tamer jumped up, eyes angry, body ready. "What's that supposed to mean, Whitey?"

Bullet was ready, if he wanted to try a fight. They stood there in the silent air, yards apart, facing off.

"The way I see it," Tamer said carefully, the words coming out slow and calculated, like a glove across the face, his eyes fixing Bullet, his heavy eyebrows low, "if you can get me to quit, you'll be able to run. Having it all your own way again."

Stupid. "I wouldn't waste my time."

Tamer stepped toward him, fists bunched. "What does that mean? You're so damned laconic, Tillerman, I don't think you know what you mean half the time you open your mouth."

"I know," Bullet said, slow and calculated, "exactly what I mean."

Tamer halted, and thought. "So you mean you wouldn't waste your time scheming like that?"

"You got it."

Tamer thought again. "You could say that, you know? Make it a little easier on the rest of us to figure out what you mean."

Bullet shrugged.

"What're you after, Tillerman?"

"I run," Bullet answered.

Tamer almost exploded. Bullet could see him belting himself in from exploding. Then he laughed, without humor: "Don't break your back being communicative. I guess, if it's a mug's game and I learn something, I'm not the mug."

"It's got nothing to do with who's a mug, Shipp," Bullet told him patiently.

"Maybe not. If you're straight; which I doubt. Whitey has trouble being straight. But that's beside the point, so keep your hair on. The point is, what good you can do me? Right?" Bullet didn't answer. "And what you just advised me, in your ineluctably supportive manner, is that I can run through it."

Ineluctably? Shit. "Yeah." Bullet drifted back toward the track.

"Do you run through it?" Tamer demanded.

"Sure."

"When?"

"Just before nine. But—" Bullet stopped himself.

"But what, Whitey?" the voice challenged him.

"I've never seen you do it."

"You've never seen me quit."

"So what?"

Tamer chewed on that. Bullet waited.

"Whadda you mean, run through it?" Tamer asked.

Bullet shrugged. "Just what it says."

Tamer groaned.

Bullet looked at him. *Coloreds give up easier, against the odds.*

"Go ahead," Tamer said, ready. "Say it."

Bullet wasn't scared. "Coloreds give up easier," he said.

"Blacks," Tamer corrected him. "And *I* don't."

You can't prove that by me.

"I've got to go now, but you can watch me tomorrow," Tamer said.

"It's still light," Bullet pointed out.

"Yeah, but I've got a job to get to."

The next afternoon, Bullet watched: watched the point of exhaustion, watched the legs and arms start to sag, watched Tamer pace down and gather himself together—and run through it. *Hunh,* he thought, watching the big muscles work. Surprised.

At the finish, Tamer fell onto the ground, as always, but his eyes were open and his teeth showed a big smile. "Brother," he said. "Bro-ther. I hate to admit it, but you were right."

Bullet didn't say anything.

"It sure does hurt, though." He looked up at Bullet, squinting against the sun. "You do that every day?"

"Yeah."

"You must feel no pain, no pain a-tall."

He could think what he liked.

"This meet tomorrow, what do you think our chances are?" Tamer got up, dusting himself off.

"Why do you keep collapsing at the finish?" Bullet asked.

"I'm not hung up on pride, not me," Tamer told him. "Whites get hung up on pride. Me, I fall down because it feels so good to be lying there. Are you telling me you don't want to do just that?"

That was the last thing Bullet wanted to do. He didn't say anything. Tamer looked at him, considering. Bullet looked right back, not considering anything.

Tamer came in third in the cross-country, an easy, level, three-mile course. The coach came over to them, elated. He started clapping them both on the back. "A week and a half of work, and already—we got it, boys; we got it in our hands. I knew you two would make an unbeatable team. I knew it." Bullet looked up to find Tamer staring right at him, his dark eyebrows raised in tolerant amusement—what the coach didn't know wouldn't hurt him, Bullet guessed.

When Jackson grabbed his shoulder and told him to eat with them in the lunchroom on Monday, Bullet thought he was in for some long speeches about "doing the right thing." He considered heading outside to eat, but not seriously: It was cold, a real edge to the wind. Not as bad as yesterday out on the water, hauling up on the oyster tongs, but not comfortable by any stretch of the imagination. So he slid onto the bench beside Lou, who did not move far enough along to give him much room. "Hi," she said, her voice low, close. "It's been a while."

Across from them Cheryl said, "I didn't miss him."

"You see him every day in History," Lou said.

"Whoopeedo," Cheryl said. "So, what do you think of Tommy's editorial?" she asked Bullet.

"I didn't read it." Bullet glanced at Tommy, who seemed to be carrying around some subdued excitement.

"You're the only one then. I got hauled over the coals by our esteemed advisor."

"Why?"

"Because the silly twit didn't know until someone told her that there was more to it than met her eye," Jackson told him. "And my guess is, they told her at some length. I could almost feel sorry for her. Except she figured that Tommy here was some tame little editor, which shows how much she knows."

"It was a good one," Tommy told Bullet, proud.

"Really good," Cheryl seconded the opinion. Bullet didn't doubt it. "'Crisfield Colors'—that's a great title too. The whole thing is great."

"Not great," Tommy said, one eye on Bullet. "But good. Great may be the one in this week's issue. See, I talked about the colors as if I was talking about red and white, but I was really—if you read it another way—talking about black and white. And she didn't pick up on it, she put her fat blue okay right on the top of the paper. I couldn't believe it, I tell you. I almost took it back and asked her if she knew what she was doing."

"They're going to keep closer tabs on you now, though," Jackson warned.

"There's nothing they can do, because we're the ones who do layout and deliver it to the printer, so we're the ones who really decide what goes in. I never thought of that before. So I've got a dummy editorial to give her this week, and I'll print the one I want to. What do you think, Bullet?"

"Sounds like you can pull it off."

"Yep. I can't believe I never realized that before. I mean, how dumb can you get? And I figure, once it's printed—what can they do? I mean, I'm an elected officer, right? They wouldn't dare just fire me. If they try to throw me out of school, I'll appeal to the school board, and they wouldn't like the publicity one bit."

"They could have you impeached," Cheryl told him.

"They could try," Tommy said, "but they'd never pull it off. Well, what do you think?" he asked Bullet.

"You look like you're enjoying yourself."

Tommy laughed over Cheryl's exasperated, "Deadhead."

"I am, we all are, aren't we? At least we're doing something, not just sitting around letting them steamroll us. Wait'll you see it, Bullet, it's called 'A Buried Incident.' About that black guy getting beat up. You gotta read it."

Bullet ate away at his sandwiches.

"Seriously, I really want you to read it. You'll like it—because whether you know it or not, you're on our side."

"He's not on anyone's side except his own," Cheryl said.

Tommy and Lou shook their heads, disagreeing. Bullet didn't bother responding. He didn't mind if Cheryl was right, for a change; it was no skin off his nose.

That afternoon he started looking at Tamer's technique. He watched him practice the hurdles and even ran one round against him. Bullet lost time over the jumps, but made it up on the runs between. As he went around the track, he no longer lost as much time and he made up even more, so that he came in well ahead at the end. "What're you trying to prove, Tillerman?" Tamer demanded.

That gets through to you, does it? Bullet wasn't pleased or displeased by the guy's anger, just interested. "Nothing, Shipp," he answered, moving on to put in a few high jumps, so the coach wouldn't get on his back. Tamer watched him go but didn't have anything to say about it. After practice, Bullet told him, "You're making some mistakes when you run. In technique."

The dark eyes stared at him, hostile. Not his problem.

"You lean too far forward," Bullet said. "You got to keep your back straighter—give your lungs a chance. And *use* your arms. You let them too loose, you know?"

"No, I don't know."

"Look, if you pump with your arms, like this—not too much, just enough—you can set your own pace up. And your knees, get them higher. You're okay with that but you could do better."

The guy just stood there, staring out from under his heavy eyebrows.

"What makes you the expert, Tillerman?"

Bullet shrugged. It made no difference to him. "Nothing. Shipp."

"And don't call me that."

"What, Shipp? It's your name."

"It's my old man's name."

"Same thing."

"No, it isn't. Not at all the same. He died bad," Tamer said.

Bullet almost laughed, and he went ahead and said what he was thinking: "And my old man lives bad. Big deal. Tough luck."

The dark face glowered at him. "I don't even want to understand you, Whitey. But I guess I better try it your way, although I don't know why I should. You're no expert and I do okay my own way. But I'll try." He went around the track, slowly. Bullet could see him reminding himself to get his back straighter, get his arms working for him. Bullet watched, not thinking about anything. Tamer went around the track again, faster this time, but not at his best speed. *Looks right,* Bullet thought. "Looks right," he called, as Tamer started off on a third round.

Coming off the track at the end of that lap, Tamer reported, "It feels right too, I am sorry to say. I can't do much about the knees, I don't think."

Bullet didn't much care. "What do I call you then?" he asked.

"You don't have to call me anything. But my name's Tamer."

The names coloreds give their kids, Bullet thought.

"Spit it out," Tamer told him.

"What kind of a name's that?" Bullet said.

Unexpectedly, the guy grinned. "You're asking me that? You—Bullet. Bul-let," Tamer said, "and you're asking *me*? You whites are something else."

So what, Bullet thought, angry. Then the humor of it struck him, and he looked over Tamer's shoulder to the track, to keep himself from smiling. "Okay," he said, looking back at the dark face, "I see what you mean. But I named myself, when I was a kid. I chose my own name."

"My mother was hoping I'd be tamer than my brothers, or at least that's what she told me."

"Yeah? Did it work?"

"Not according to her. But I am civilized, a civilized man. What's your real name?"

"Bullet," Bullet told him. "They named me Samuel."

"After the prophet in the Bible?" Bullet had no idea. "Man, do parents ever not know, yeah?" Tamer remarked. "They just dream all over their kids. All that wishing and hoping—it's really sad if you think about it."

Bullet never thought about it.

"And I'm as guilty as the next man," Tamer said.

"Hunh?"

"You didn't know? That's right, I forgot—information doesn't cross the color barrier. I've got a kid, a baby girl."

"Why'd you do that?" Bullet demanded.

Tamer laughed. He laughed so hard he had to lean against a tree to stay standing up. "The usual reason," he choked out. "Don't get pissed, I know what you meant—but you heard how it sounded. C'mon, Bullet, no need to feel ashamed, nobody heard you but me, just some black guy. And it's funny," he laughed.

Bullet had to admit it was.

"But I'm not about to let you know what we named her, un-unh," Tamer said. "Because then you *would* laugh. And I'll answer the question, yes, I'm married—well, it was my fault as well as hers, and yes it cost me the year of school. Whitey wasn't getting me onto welfare."

"Most coloreds don't feel that way," Bullet said.

"Blacks," Tamer said. "And you don't know from nothing about it, Whitey."

The next afternoon an icy rain drizzled down from the low clouds, so the coach cut practice short. Bullet and Tamer stayed behind to practice. Three of the other runners, all white, stayed behind too. "Hey, Bullet, the coach said we should see if you'd give us some tips," their spokesman said. "Would you?" They were sure of his answer, they were ready to do what he said.

"No," Bullet said. *Not worth my time.*

"Hunh?" Surprise stopped them. "Why not?"

Bullet didn't say anything.

"What's so special about him?"

Bullet didn't say anything. He'd never thought about it, except he wasn't wasting his time with Tamer. And he knew these three.

"What is it, you turning into a nigger lover? Inte-*gra*-tionist liberal?"

"Black," Tamer corrected patiently.

"No," Bullet said.

"Shipp?" they asked Tamer.

Nothing to do with him. What were they trying? *Nobody can make me.*

"You asking me to put pressure on him? On *him*? You're asking a nigger for help? You're in a bad way, Whitey. A bad way."

"How come he'll work with you and not us?"

"Damn-all if I know," Tamer said. "Who knows why he does anything. But I can tell you, it's no picnic. So if I were you, I'd tell the coach you don't want to anymore. Think about it before you fly off the handle. We're doing better, aren't we? If you want to get a shot at the state championships, you can't afford to have Bullet off the team again, can you?"

"Okay," they muttered. "Yeah. Okay. I didn't want to do this anyway, did you? Work with that bastard?"

They went off to the showers and Tamer turned to Bullet. "They had me scared for a minute. There's only so much integration I plan to tolerate."

“They didn’t scare me,” Bullet said. “Doesn’t it burn you?”

“Them?” Tamer asked. “Are you kidding? Besides, you were burned enough to cover the situation for both of us and have some left over.” He started off around the cross-country trail, taking it a little slow to keep his back straight, to get his arms working and his legs in sync. Bullet stayed at the track, going over the hurdles, concentrating on footwork as he approached each jump. His timing was still off. Once he figured that out, he thought, he’d work on the angle of his following leg as he went over the jumps. *First things first.*

CHAPTER 18

As they left History class on Thursday morning, Cheryl handed Bullet a copy of the school paper. "Take a look at the editorial," she told him, then added, "If you can read. This one'll really get them going. I can barely wait to see what they do about it—he's really nailed them on this one."

Bullet read it at the start of the next class, opening the six-page paper to the editorial page and folding it back before putting it on his desktop.

A Buried Incident
—for Tamer Shipp

They discovered the incident one morning, going to work. There were a few of them who came upon it simultaneously, all of them wearing light gray suits and carrying the rules rolled up in their pockets, sticking out; all of them with polished shoes, their shoelaces tied into neat, manly bows.

The incident looked terrible, lying there on the roadside. It was almost unrecognizable. Was it black? a little black incident? Or was it white, a white one? Or red? Or blue?

Nasty, they knew it was nasty. They took the rules out of their pockets and unrolled them. For a long time they tried to find out what the rules told them to do, because what the rules said wasn't what they wanted to do. Then for a long time they stood, all around, looking down at the disgusting little incident, which was just lying there. They really wanted to go away and pretend they hadn't seen it, pretend they had gone to work down the other road that morning, or driven by so important and fast they couldn't possibly have noticed.

"What if?" one said. And "What if?" another answered. "What if?" "What if?" So they pushed it out of sight and buried it in the dirt by the wayside, covering it over with leaves. The first thing they did when they got to work was wash their hands. "Phew," they said. "That was close." "Phew."

The buried incident rotted peacefully away, until the children came along. Curious, the way children are, and not knowing any better, they pushed the leaves away and dug around in the dirt, until they could see what it was. "Ugh," they said. "I don't like it." "I don't want it." Some of them vomited. Some of them poked at it with sticks to show how brave and clever they were. Scientific-minded children picked up little pieces of it to take home and study. Bullies threw stones at it. A few girls cried a few tears.

When the men walked past in the evening they could see that the grave had been tampered with. "Where is the dog who has done this?" they demanded in big voices. "Mad dog." "Animal control." "Rabies," they called out.

And the incident rose up, its bones strung together, its half-rotten flesh even harder to identify. The buried incident rose up, crawled out of its grave and waved its arms at them.

Bullet returned the paper to Cheryl as she went into the lunchroom. She looked surprised to have it put back into her hands. "Thanks," he said. She added it to the pile she was carrying to pass out. As he went by the table where Tommy sat, Bullet stopped to say, "Not bad."

Tommy smiled happily up at him. "You're just jealous." He looked pleased with himself. Somebody called Tommy's name and Bullet moved on, to sit with the wimps. He watched the groups by Tommy's table, all during lunch. People, both black and white, came by to say things that made Tommy smile.

* * *

That afternoon, Bullet ran a couple of times around the course beside Tamer, keeping his own pace easy but stretching Tamer's. Tamer ran it twice more on his own while Bullet worked over the hurdles. Tamer watched the end of that. "You want some advice?" he offered, as Bullet finished a round.

Bullet shook his head: he was concentrating on trying to feel down his muscles what was wrong; he was getting too much height and not enough forward movement in the jumps.

"Come off it, Tillerman." Tamer faced him. "Is it that important to you always to be in top position?"

"Hunh?"

"I do know something about hurdling," Tamer said.

Coloreds, always thinking you were putting them down.

"I won't tell anybody," Tamer said, sarcastic.

"Can it," Bullet said, not angry for a wonder. "It doesn't work for me that way. I do it. Until it feels right."

"Nobody can teach *you*, is that it?"

"Yeah." *That's it exactly.*

The heavy eyebrows lowered.

"You can get steamed if you want to, if you want to take it personally. For the record, though, I don't care what position I'm in. I have never worried myself about that."

Tamer just stared at him. "I think you're straight," he finally said.

Of course I am.

"Then what if I ran a few? My technique is pretty good—I had some good coaching before. You want me to do that?"

Bullet nodded. Tamer chuckled, shrugged, loped onto the track and ran the hurdles slowly, easily. Bullet watched his approach to the jumps, how he distanced himself to take off, the forward angle of his torso as he went over it. Bullet could feel that, that leaning forward into the landing. He hadn't been doing that. Before Tamer finished, he went back to the start. *Get off sooner than you think*, he told himself. He took down a couple of hurdles at the beginning, but he held the picture of Tamer's jumps in his mind and he could feel how that worked.

"Yeah," he said to the big colored guy.

"You're welcome," Tamer answered, sarcastic again. "Are you going to be running the hurdles? Frankly, I hope not," he added.

"Naw," Bullet told him. "Running on a track—I don't like it. You know?"

"No, I don't. But, as I see it, that's your problem."

"You got it," Bullet agreed. "You're looking better over the hurdles," he remarked.

"Yeah, I am. It feels better too. After cross-country, the hurdles is a breeze. I like that. You know, I originally planned, when we moved down here—I was going to play football. It's what I played before. It's easier to look good for scholarship money with football. College," he explained to Bullet's expression. "You've heard the phrase, going to college."

"I seem to remember it from somewhere."

"But I'm not playing football. . . ."

"I heard."

"And I was burned about that. But being burned doesn't do any good, so I figured track was my next best bet. A real second-rater though, I thought. Now, I don't know. I've been thinking, like Hamlet says, there's a divinity that shapes our ends. You know? It's Shakespeare."

"I've heard of him," Bullet told Tamer. "My father used to quote him at me—when he used to speak to me. 'How sharper than a serpent's tooth it is to have a thankless child,'" he proved.

"My old man quoted the racing form, when he wasn't too strung out to do more than dribble where he sat," Tamer said. "Tough luck, yeah?"

"Yeah."

"The way I see it now, track'll do me as well as football. Maybe better. I'm pretty good. Not like you, not in your class, not anywhere near your class. But better than most, which is good enough. Much better than most."

"What does that matter?" Bullet wondered.

"Brother, I can hold down two jobs and still get through high school with no trouble and top grades. But I doubt that I can do that in college, not with a family to support. Not the kind of jobs I can get. I need a good scholarship."

"What jobs you do?"

"This year? I wash dishes at a place on the road up to Salisbury, a truck stop. And pump gas up to Route Fifty on weekends, the night shifts. Both minimum wage, which is very minimum, let me tell you. The time's no big hassle now, but I'm hoping the academic standards at college will be a little higher."

"I wouldn't know."

"And don't intend to find out, if I'm right. Am I right?"

"So what?"

"Hey—so nothing. It's none of my business. I'm not even much interested."

He meant that, Bullet could see; he knew how to leave people alone. *Coloreds grow up faster,* he thought.

"Say it."

"You're grown up," Bullet said.

"My guess is I always was," Tamer told him. "But not because I'm black, don't kid yourself about that."

Colored, Bullet corrected.

An all-school meeting was called for the next morning, first period. The students filed into the auditorium by homerooms, the youngest nearest the front and seniors at the back. Jackson, who was in Bullet's homeroom, slouched down in his chair next to Bullet and leaned over to remark, "The shit has truly hit the fan. Just what we expected, right?"

Bullet didn't answer.

"This'll be fun," Jackson decided.

Once the students were settled, the administrative officers filed onto the stage and took their seats in a long row at the center of the stage, behind the podium where a microphone had been set up. The principal stood at the microphone, with the three assistant principals behind him, as well as the school supervisor, and the heads of departments with their blue gradebooks and gray attendance books on their laps. The rest of the teachers sat at the end-row seats. A few stood by the two sets of doors leading into the auditorium. The adults watched the students, their eyes roving over the noisy auditorium, looking for signs of trouble, keeping guard.

The principal cleared his throat, waited for silence to fall and started to speak. His voice, magnified by the microphone, came at them from speakers mounted along the wall. "Boys and girls," he said.

Bullet settled back. He might as well get a little sleep, or try to.

"I am sure that you have a good idea about why I've called this assembly. I hope you will forgive me for making it impossible for you to get to your first-period classes. . . ." He waited for a ripple of laughter that did not appear. Bullet opened his eyes: It might be interesting after all.

"I have decided that the best way to deal with a problem we all face—do you hear that? We all face it, it is a problem for all of us. The best way to deal with it is in a public hearing. That is the purpose for which we are gathered here this morning. Let me begin by calling up to the stage Thomas Leeds. Thomas?"

Tommy got up from a seat in the front row among the eighth-graders. He looked clean and neat and composed; he'd known this was going to happen. Beside Bullet, Jackson clapped his hands, loudly and slowly, all the time Tommy was getting up on stage. Nobody else made any sound.

Tommy stopped a few feet away from the podium and the principal. Jackson stopped clapping. Tommy let his arms hang at his sides for a few seconds. He shoved his hands into the pockets of his khakis. He took them out and put them behind his back. The principal waited. Tommy shifted his weight from leg to leg.

Finally the principal turned back to the microphone. "Most of you already know Thomas, but at the risk of being repetitive, I'll introduce him. Thomas is the editor of our school newspaper, *The Crimson Blade.* He was elected last spring to this position, elected by you. The faculty approved the election. The faculty felt, as you obviously did, that Thomas was worthy of the responsibility his position gave him. We all felt we could trust Thomas to represent all of our opinions fairly to the public.

"Do you think I'm being foolish to mention the public? Remember, boys and girls, that at this time in history, any public school is in everyone's eyes. We are all responsible, especially at this time, responsible not only to ourselves and every high school student across the entire country, but also responsible to future generations. The hard fact is that what we do today will determine how the future generation of school children—black and white—will find the institutions we leave to them. It is no small decision you will make here today, boys and girls."

So they were going to try to get him voted out. Well, it was a bold enough move, and pretty smart. Tommy had struck out at them and this was the counterattack. It made sense.

"This is America, a democracy, and Thomas has been duly elected to his position of responsibility. We"—he turned to make a gesture that included the adults sitting in a quiet row behind him—"are seriously concerned about Thomas's use of this position. We are also, however, serious in our respect for anyone whom you have voted into office. We respect your votes. Therefore, we have decided we all need a hearing, where each side can present its case. At the end of this, we will ask you to vote again, in your homerooms. The decision will be announced at lunchtime and we pledge ourselves to stand by it, whatever it is."

The audience shifted in its seats. Bullet wondered if Tommy had figured that they would be so clever in their response.

"Thomas? You should, I think, be allowed to speak first. Are you ready to present your views?"

That surprised Tommy. He hadn't expected that. But he stepped up to the podium. "My views are pretty simple," he said. Magnified, the nervousness in his voice made him sound much less believable than the more practiced speaker beside him. "First, I think I have told the truth." He hesitated, waiting for some other words to come to him. "I think that's important, to tell the truth. Really important. The truth is important." He stopped himself. "Okay, second, I believe in freedom of the press, because"—he looked down, looked around—"without that, they can tell us anything and we don't have any way of finding out the real truth." He studied his hands for a minute. "I mean, if there is no freedom of the press, then there's no way for the truth to come out. If it is being kept hidden." He waited for a few awkward seconds then said, "I guess that's all I have to say. But I really mean it."

Jackson groaned softly. Tommy stepped aside again. He started to leave the stage, but the principal told him to stay, so he stood there, a few feet back, his hands behind his back.

"Is that everything you wanted to say?" the principal asked. Tommy's flushed face nodded. "Are you sure? I don't want anyone to think we have cut you off short." Tommy nodded again.

The principal turned back to the auditorium. "It seems to us that there are some important principles involved here that have not yet been mentioned. The first is the idea of playing by the rules. For all the years I can remember, there has been a well-known rule that all articles for the paper are reviewed and approved by a faculty advisor. Since the school is ultimately held responsible for everything that appears in the newspaper—and by school in this case I mean the school officials—it seems only fair that this rule should be respected. Your editor has not done this, which constitutes a serious breach of faith. The editorial in question was deliberately *not* shown to the advisor. In fact a false editorial was given to her for her approval. That isn't a misrepresentation of the facts, is it, Thomas?"

Tommy shook his head.

"Now, whatever my personal feelings about such underhanded methods, or about dealing with someone who is deliberately hypocritical—such a breach of trust of the position, trust placed by you, should not go unnoted.

"Second, we are, as you well know, at a critical time in our nation's history. It is all too easy to destroy, in the unconsidered heat of the moment, what it has taken generations to build. We must, especially at this difficult time, be able to take the long view. We must, all of us, think not about our immediate needs or feelings, but about the greater good, the higher purpose. The greater good is peaceful and full integration of the colors, so that each man and woman can be genuinely equal among his fellows. The higher purpose—well, education is our purpose here, to give you the tools you will need to be able to become self-supporting as well as to function as responsible citizens of the democracy that nourishes us all.

"It is easy—too easy—to inflame an already dangerous situation. Nothing is easier. It is easy to take advantage of the feelings of others, to stir others up to fever pitch. It is especially easy for a young man of talent to do so—and Thomas is a young man of talent, or else you would not have honored him with the position he holds. But how has he used his talent and position?

"I am personally saddened by this, because unlike some of our unfortunate neighbors to the west, this high school has been spared much of the destructive effects of what is going on around the country."

Tommy seemed to wake up and become agitated. "Hey, hang on," he said.

"Excuse me, Thomas, you have had your time to speak. I would prefer not to be interrupted."

Helpless, Tommy withdrew into silence.

"I will mention only one example. The hallways at Anne Arundel County schools have police guards stationed in them. Is this what you want to happen here? Policemen with trained attack dogs are put on duty at all sporting events. Do you want that to happen to your school? Teachers are leaving their jobs, without notice, twenty-five percent of them since school opened in the fall. They cannot be replaced by able people. Is that the kind of education you want for yourselves?"

But that has nothing to do with it.

"Do you want to come to school every day, not knowing whether or not violence will erupt? That has not been the case here, and that is a credit to you, to all of you, and to your teachers. When I read the newspapers, I am proud of us all, because we are achieving what many say cannot be achieved. I think that achievement is now being threatened. This saddens me and frightens me."

Bullet could feel the ripples of fear going around the auditorium—everybody knew that schools in many places were not safe, for teachers or students.

Tommy looked like he wanted to say something, but the principal silenced him with a glance.

"Finally, there is one more point. Like it or not, you are not adults. You do not carry adult responsibilities. You are not expected to. Students are not drafted—which is a clear statement. The adults of your community—however imperfect they may be—do their best to make your lives safe and useful."

Bullet saw now what the man was doing. He was using the assembly to make sure Tommy got voted out of his job. He had put Tommy up there on stage where he'd be nervous and not look good. He had let Tommy talk first because people would remember most clearly whatever was said last; then he had taken out all of his heavy ammunition to attack with. This was supposed to be a hearing, but it was more like a seige. At first, the army outside had been the adults on stage, surrounding the students with their authority. Now, as the principal talked, everybody but Tommy was in the army outside, lying in wait to get through the walls. Tommy seemed to have figured out the position, but he couldn't do anything about it.

Well, Tommy had brought it all about by his own choice, Bullet thought. On the other hand, the principal hadn't ever talked about the truth of the editorial. He had talked about other things, using fear and patriotism, and even pride, to get people thinking his way. He was obscuring the supposed cause, which was whether or not they had done a cover-up on the incident, whether or not things were as peaceful and safe as they said. It was nothing more than a seige, and it was going to be one of the shortest seiges on record, Bullet thought, because Tommy didn't seem to realize where his best defense lay.

"You must be careful not to react like children in a tantrum, screaming and biting. A truly mature young person understands that when wiser heads than his cannot reduce a problem to simplicity, he must respect the difficulty of the problem. It is that maturity, so essential to an editor—"

Bullet stood up and pushed his way over the knees of the people in his row toward the center aisle. He would have gone for the side aisle, which was less obtrusive, but the teacher sitting there would have stopped him. He turned to walk up and out.

"Samuel Tillerman." The name echoed from all the loudspeakers. Bullet turned around. "May I ask what you are doing?"

The principal was trying to set it up, the way he had set up Tommy. Bullet met his eyes but didn't answer. He figured what he was doing was self-evident.

"You're leaving?" the man finally asked.

Bullet nodded. You could see the guy trying to figure out how to handle this.

"Why are you leaving?"

The guy was scared everybody would get up and follow Bullet out. Bullet didn't give two hoots about everybody. Or even about Tommy. He just wasn't about to stay there any longer and be lied at. "You said this was a hearing," he called back, down the broad aisle and up onto the stage. "It isn't," he said.

"I see," the voice said. "What is it then?"

You know exactly what it is.

The principal misunderstood Bullet's silence. "Sit down, Samuel," he ordered.

Bullet just stood there, for a while, then turned around again. He didn't hurry up the aisle, didn't go slow; he moved along at his usual pace.

"Samuel? I think your days among us are numbered," the voice threatened him.

The really big gun—expulsion.

Bullet turned at the door to answer. "Yes, I expect they are." *With one hundred eighty school days in a year, they were always numbered.*

He waited, to see if the guy had anything else he wanted to say, not nervous, not uncomfortable, just waiting. He didn't care, and that seemed to sink in after a while—he didn't care about the principal up on the stage, or about Tommy up there blowing it, or about the students sitting turned in their seats to watch him. None of them could make him do anything, and he knew it. After a while that seemed to sink in. So he left the auditorium.

Nobody said anything to him about walking out. Everybody was too wrapped up in discussions of the results of the vote. Once these were announced in the cafeteria, everybody started talking about who the new editor would be. Nobody seemed to notice that the next editor was going to be appointed by the faculty committee instead of elected. Everybody was just busy deciding whether or not to try for the job. "Well, it looks so good on your college applications," Cheryl apologized to Tommy. "And I know I'm not popular, but the faculty likes me."

"Go ahead," Tommy told her. "You're welcome to it. You'll look good with a brown nose."

Cheryl walked away.

"I can't believe they did this to me," Tommy said to Bullet, waving his hand to indicate the people all over the lunchroom. "Jerks. I looked bad though."

Bullet didn't disagree. He wondered if Tommy realized that his editorial had been no more favorable to the students than to the administration—a truly unbiased piece. What did Tommy expect?

"He outmaneuvered me."

And how.

"I seriously underestimated the man. Oh hell, who cares anyway. I've got better things to do with my time than try to make a rinky-ding school newspaper look good. But I wish I had your guts, Bullet."

You wish you had won the vote.

Somebody came over and put a hand on Tommy's shoulder. "Tough luck."

"Yeah, it's a pisser," Tommy said, without heat.

Only two people said anything to Bullet about what he'd done. The first was the coach, who came hustling over at the start of practice, his windbreaker zipped to his throat against the cold. Bullet knew what was bugging him, the state championships.

"Do us a favor, Tillerman, don't get yourself thrown out of school before December. Will you do that? Will you just try to do that?"

"Sure," Bullet said. *The team has worked so hard,* he predicted.

"Because the rest of the guys have all worked so hard," the coach said.

You owe it to the team.

"It wouldn't be fair for you to let them down now."

The second person was Tamer, which surprised Bullet. Tamer didn't even wait until after they had worked out. "You lost it," he said, angry.

Hunh?

"Why'd you do that, Bullet? You could have said just about anything, and everybody in that auditorium would have gotten up to follow you out. They were just looking for a reason. Just waiting to be shown what they suspected. What's wrong with you?"

Not a thing. Not anything you mean anyway. "Are we going to work or not?" Bullet demanded. It was nothing to do with Tamer.

"Don't give me that. You were standing there, and there was nothing, but nothing, he could do to you. You had the whole place right in your hand. You saw right through him, you got right to the real point—if you'd explained anything, just to make it clear. You can't expect people to think for themselves. And there's your real equality, neither blacks nor whites are doing much thinking. But someone like you, all you've got to do is show them how you see things. I would have been the first one up myself—I thought about doing it anyway, but until you explained what he was up to it would have been just a black activist gesture, it wouldn't have counted for anything. What did you *want*, Bullet?"

"I wanted to get out of there."

"Don't you care that you could have had everybody behind you?"

"No."

Tamer stared at him, studying his face.

"Are we going to do any work? I am, whether you do or not."

"You really don't care, do you? You don't make any connections, you haven't got any." Tamer didn't expect an answer, didn't wait for one. "I don't understand you, Tillerman. You're not cut out for ordinary life—you know that? I'm not putting you down, I'm just figuring something out. I don't know what's going to happen to you. You're either going to end up really great or dead."

"Everybody ends up dead," Bullet pointed out.

"No, you know what I mean. Dead young, dead with your life wasted—because you're going to drop out, aren't you?"

No need to answer that.

"And they'll draft you, which you won't mind—and if you survive you'll be some kind of five-star general, chief of staff. With your potential. How can you waste that potential, Bullet? Think of what you could achieve."

Coloreds—and all the liberal types too—always thinking about making the world a better place.

"Or destroy," Tamer continued. "I don't know what you are.

Some kind of loner. I never met anyone at all like you. I'd like to have you on our side though. If you ever decide to connect up with anything."

Coloreds, always making it one side or the other.

"Say it."

"You coloreds, you always turn it into taking sides."

"Blacks," Tamer snapped.

"And why do you always do that anyway, what's it matter?" Bullet demanded.

"Blacks is our name for ourselves. Not something laid on us by anybody else. Of anyone, you should understand that."

I never thought, Bullet thought.

CHAPTER 19

Walker was reciting another Housman poem to them. He was doing it because they had ten minutes to spare, and this was a poem about history, he told them. Bullet was willing to listen—chances were that Housman might be worth listening to. There had only been one jerkwater remark; most of the class had learned its lesson that last time he started talking poetry. But somebody had to say, "This isn't English class."

"No, it isn't," Walker agreed pleasantly. Nothing got his goat. "See if you can make the connection," he asked them.

The poem was full of names nobody knew, Wenlock and Wrekin, Uricon the city; about Romans and Englishmen and at the end the Roman was dead, had been dead for a long time, and the city was ashes.

"Okay," Walker said to the puzzled class. "Do you know about the Roman occupation of England?" They didn't. "It was about the time of Caesar, about nineteen hundred years ago. The Roman legions conquered Britain. They stayed there, occupying it, for a couple of hundred years, occupying troops. Housman wrote this poem in the early years of this century. Now, listen again."

Bullet listened: There was a storm blowing around the woods. Housman was saying that it was just like the storms that blew hundreds of years ago, "the old wind in the old anger."

Bullet liked that line. Housman talked about a young Roman and said they were alike. He meant, although he didn't say it straight out, that the same storm was blowing through him, right then. Then he said the storm in the woods would soon be done, would blow away.

Walker let it sink in for a minute, then told them: "Historical lesson number one. While events change, the human creature doesn't. Because the gale of life blows through you, doesn't it? Your blood warms you, you have thoughts that hurt." Nobody wanted to talk about that, although nobody disagreed. They didn't want to talk just because they didn't disagree.

Walker didn't make them, didn't seem to want to make them. "Lesson number two—a great abstraction—all that really lasts of history is—I hate to use this word but there's nothing better: art. Song and story, picture and statue. The mosaic floor of a Roman villa in England. This poem. The golden death mask of Agamemnon. Thomas Jefferson's home, Monticello. These are the real fruits of history, these are the enduring fruits.

"And lesson number three, which is the tough one. You have to live in some connection between these two irreconcilable ideas." He looked around and apparently saw the confusion. "Okay, don't worry about that one. Just worry about gathering the fruits, do that, and the rest will follow. Wait, maybe the rest will follow. If you even just try to remember, it's effectively the same thing."

"What are you telling us? Why are you talking like this?" Cheryl asked him.

"Because I think you are young at a difficult time in time," he said.

Nobody argued with that.

"I'm trying to give you . . ." Walker smiled, pale and as wimpy as his beard. ". . . the benefit of my vast years of education, passing on to you the ancient wisdom." His tone was self-mocking and the class responded with mock groans.

"Besides," Walker added, "it's worth making a fool of myself to see Mr. Tillerman wake up during class."

Bullet didn't respond to that. Besides, the bell was ringing. Besides he liked that line, "the old wind in the old anger." He didn't give two hoots about Romans or art, but he liked that old wind and old anger. He didn't even mind Walker using him to get people smiling; it was nothing but the truth after all.

The meet that Saturday was the second to last. This one was held over near the Delaware line, against another high school pretty much like theirs. The Warriors cleaned up on that one, taking seconds in high jump and the one hundred meter, but first in everything else. Bullet even took a first in the javelin with one hundred and sixteen feet. It wasn't much of a match. There were a couple of interesting points, though. Tamer came in within one and a half seconds of the present high school record on the hurdles, and the coach's eyes lit up like he was about to explode. For a while he just paced incoherently around in a small circle, hitting at his thigh with his fist. "You look good, Shipp," he said. He slapped Tamer on the back. "You look good." They were all standing around together, waiting for the relay race to begin. Their runners were on the track, the four of them, two black and two white, spread around the oval. "I'm beginning to believe in this," the coach said. "How's it feel, Shipp? Tillerman? How's it feel to collect the fruits of your labors." He didn't wait for any answer. "We have got ourselves a team that can compete," he rejoiced.

They took the relay, too.

* * *

On the next Thursday, Bullet made his way through the lunch tables to find one that was empty. Except for a couple of wimps engaged in a game of chess on a tiny little board they had set up between their lunch trays. The pieces were so little they knocked them over whenever they moved one. They looked up at him with big eyes and shifted down a little to give him all the room he wanted.

Pete, with Ted Bayson, nodding and smiling behind him, and Lou with her arm draped over Ted's shoulder, called across to Bullet: "You guys gonna look as good this week?"

"If we had a meet we would," Bullet told them. He unwrapped his peanut butter sandwiches and drank down some milk. Tommy put his tray down across from him. "Hey, Bullet," he said. "Hey, Larry, Zach." The chess players nodded abstractedly.

"So, what's new?" Tommy asked Bullet.

Bullet chewed, swallowed.

"See who's with Ted now?"

"Yeah."

"I guess she goes for you strong, silent types. You think? Only she likes them with hair." Bullet grinned. Tommy always did like lipping off. "But that means Meredith's available—and in need of comfort. You want to comfort her? Naw, you never looked twice at any female. So it's up to me. Women, who needs 'em, right? Cheryl stole my material, did you see? About the draft, my crab metaphor idea. Did you read this week's *Blade*?"

"No."

"That's my man," Tommy approved. He picked up the plastic knife and fork to start on his slices of turkey, swimming in the same gravy that covered the scoop of mashed potatoes, the scoop of stuffing and the scoop of corn. "I almost didn't read it either, but I couldn't resist the temptation to see what the twerps were up to. The more I think about it, the better off I think I am, out of it. My God, the hours of work. And for what? What does a lousy school paper matter. It's not going to make any difference at all to the fate of the world—right?"

True enough.

"And that's not sour grapes," Tommy told him.

Bullet didn't exactly believe that. He hoped Tommy didn't either.

"Because I never knew, until I had the time, how much better I could use my time. Listen, Bullet." He glanced quickly at the chess players, who were entirely absorbed in their game. "How would you feel if you had a chance to really do something?"

I do. I have. I did.

"I was talking to some people—I can't tell you who, but it would surprise you—and we think it's time for some action. Not any of this peaceable mass movement stuff, that's what they want us to do because then nothing changes. But—

"Can you keep a secret? What am I asking, I know you can. Torture wouldn't get something out of you you didn't want to say. But, for example, there are files and records in the office, on everybody. Which students can't see. I don't even know if teachers can see theirs. They're a little branch of the damned FBI in there."

Tommy talked on, but Bullet stopped listening. He was looking at Tommy, seeing a little kid with curly red hair and white skin that sunburned so bad he had to spend all summer in an undershirt. When you shot marbles with Tommy and you won, you could be sure he would win them back the next day, playing with grim concentration, not talking or messing around, until he counted the pile in front of him and looked up, satisfied that he was ahead again.

"And they don't even lock the door. A couple of guys, a little kerosene, and whoosh—"

Losing ate away at Tommy, like rot eating away at some vine, until he figured out how to get even. If he'd been the one to walk out of that assembly, Tommy would have felt all right about himself, but he never fought back openly. And now he was talking about incendiaries.

"What are you after, Tommy?" Bullet asked.

"Two things, really," Tommy answered eagerly. "First to get rid of their records . . ." And he was off, about the kinds of records and the kinds of uses they were put to. Bullet looked at him, at the way his long bright hair straggled around his face and his cheeks looked bony and his eyes were bitter. What had happened to Tommy?

Growing up. What happened to all of them. Tough luck. Bullet wanted to lean across to Tommy, lean across the years, really, and yell at him. "You don't have to be like this, you've got other choices; at least tell yourself the truth, nobody can make you lie to yourself." He jammed the wax paper back into the brown bag, angry, ready to move away.

". . . including their suspicions, if they think you're on dope or anything . . ." Tommy talked on.

But why should Bullet be angry? Because he knew Tommy wouldn't listen, wouldn't hear. So what? What did Tommy matter anyway; he'd known for years how different they were, how different they'd gotten. What did he want from Tommy? He wanted— He stopped himself, then moved his brain slowly forward again. *No compromising,* he reminded himself. Because Patrice was right about him. He wanted Tommy to be as good as he could. And Tommy wasn't going to do that, not by a long shot. So Bullet wanted—not to care.

". . . in a court and it gets treated like holy writ and none of it's been investigated, just rumors written . . ."

And he couldn't do anything about it, not just Tommy, couldn't change anything, couldn't not care, but everybody—he couldn't make those runners want to practice as hard as they could. He couldn't make any difference, however hard he ran himself. Not to Liza, especially. She was so far away he couldn't reach far enough to connect even if he tried to. She was just out there, probably singing some song where he couldn't even hear her. He'd lost her. Okay, he could take the truth. He minded losing her, dumb old Liza with her hair like honey and her songs like spun gold. He guessed he'd have to take that truth too.

"Hey, man, are you listening to me?"

Bullet was listening to Liza, singing an old song, ". . . any stars in my crown, When at evening the sun goeth down . . ." in her molten voice.

"I don't know why I bother trying to connect with you," Tommy said. "You've been screwed up for years, Bullet. You don't care about anything."

That got Bullet's attention. *Don't I wish,* he almost wished.

"But listen to me. The other reason is, if we do that, then the blacks will know we're really on their side. Really committed . . ."

Because Tommy, and everybody in the room, was going to go out and be about a quarter of what they could be. They'd say it was because life was so tough, that was the lie they'd tell themselves. Liza wasn't so different, wasn't so bad—and Tommy couldn't even sing. They'd get old and wrinkled up like raisins and they'd think it was life's fault they'd never done what they could.

". . . white society that destroys them, gives them a second-rate education then gets on their backs for not being better educated. Makes it impossible for them to get good jobs and sometimes any job at all, then complains because they're on welfare. Did you know there are as many whites as blacks on welfare? You never hear about that, do you?"

Because they didn't like what the choices cost them. Who did? Like Tommy, he'd said he knew what it would cost printing that editorial, but when it cost that, here he was, getting even. Just the way he always had, getting back all the marbles. Bullet listened to Tommy now, because he was too sad to do anything else.

"It's just a different form of slavery. If I were black it wouldn't feel much different to me. Economic slavery and sociological slavery. I'd be pissed, if I were black."

Yeah but you're not. Because you cannot be what you are not. It was hard enough to be what you were. Easier, Bullet saw now, to pretend you were something you weren't and say if you were how you'd feel and behave, easier than working on yourself.

". . . organized around a leader. It would have to be a black, because they don't much trust us. That Shipp character they beat up, he'd be good. You hear them talk about him, they think he walks on water. But the guy's got a wife and kid, he's got jobs because they don't have much family around here to help out; he's not as useful as he could be."

Tommy's *they*s were switching around, and he didn't even hear it. He didn't want to hear it.

"I thought," Bullet said carefully, "Vietnam was your personal crusade."

"Man, I had that all wrong. This is the real war. Look around you—this room looks like a layer cake, half vanilla, half chocolate. And there's no real difference between us, except the vanilla knows how to keep the chocolate on the bottom of the pan. This is the real war, right here. This is the big one, the long one. This is the war with some future and purpose to it. And all over the color of a man's skin. To prove that white are better. To hide the fact that we're all the same."

Tommy had his hands on half the truth, because whatever the cost to Bullet personally, the Vietnam thing would end. One way or the other, win or lose. But Tommy needed the other half of the truth. "We aren't all the same," Bullet said. *Nothing is more different than each person, one from the other, every one from every other.*

People were beginning to empty out of the lunch room.

You've got to honor the differences, or what's similar will be useless to you.

"You're kidding," Tommy said. "C'mon, Bullet—you really think you're any different from the rest of us? Oh, I grant you, with that trick you have of not saying much, you look different, and you're not scared of anything, but how does that make you so damned superior? Everybody sits down to take a crap, Bullet."

So what.

"You had me fooled. I thought you were really something; I even admired you. You looked so strong, nobody could pull the wool over your eyes. I thought—last week—you were going to tell them, really let them have it. But you never were my friend, were you. You don't have friends; you don't have any connections to anybody at all. That's the only thing that bothers me, seeing through you like that. I don't give a damn about their stupid newspaper, or being editor, I don't even miss it. I don't even mind seeing how far downhill Cheryl can pull the thing in a week. But you—"

Bullet stood up. He looked down at Tommy, down across the years. "You don't have to settle for half the truth," he said.

For a second, he thought Tommy understood. Then the pale bony face closed him out. "You can't fool me," Tommy said, bitterly. "Not anymore. I didn't think you'd try. I thought better of you, Bullet."

"No, you didn't," Bullet said, meaning exactly and precisely what he said.

CHAPTER 20

That night, Bullet came into the kitchen while his parents were having their dinner. His father served onto the two plates from a platter of pork chops, a bowl of stewed tomatoes and a bowl of noodles. The old man was just starting to serve when Bullet came in. There were five chops, three for the old man, two for his mother. She used to cook pork chops up in nines, three for him, two for her, three for Bullet, and the extra one against a large appetite. The extra one always got eaten.

She used to cook platters of food, to feed all of them, her hands quick and strong, making bread, washing up, her voice sharp and quick. No matter how stony his father sat, she put all the quickness she had into that room. Until they started leaving, no more Johnny to fight back, no more Liza to go stand beside her mother with tears rolling out of her eyes. Now his mother sat as stony as his father, all her quickness gone.

Bullet walked over to the shelves. He wanted to slam his fist through the glass panes of the cupboard door. But why so angry? Because there was always nothing he could do, because Liza shouldn't have left her here like this with the two of them. Because he was going to leave too, he was going to have to leave the farm behind him and never come back. Never work his own crops out of it and make it as good as it once had been—and he could have done that, he could feel that in his back and his hands.

But he'd known for years now he was going to lose it. So why so angry?

Because he wasn't doing a damned thing for her. Couldn't. Just adding to it for her. *Too bad. Tough luck.*

No compromising, he warned himself. Because he wanted—he wanted to do something, even knowing he couldn't change anything, not the way things were, not the way things were going to be. Because he couldn't stand to be one of the things that worked to break her. He wasn't, he wouldn't be, he didn't want to do that: that could scare him, scare him cold down through his jittery bones.

I never thought, Bullet thought, knowing how he looked right then as if he could stand outside the window and see himself: straight back and shoulders stiff, chin high, face a mask, and the skin of his head bronzed. He hoped not, he hoped he wasn't, but he couldn't be sure. He just didn't know how much like his old man he was.

Thoughtfully, Bullet took a can of spaghetti out of the cupboard, opened it, scraped the coagulated mass into a pan and put it over a low flame on the stove. He left the wooden spoon in the pan. He took down a bowl and got out an eating spoon, thinking. He stirred the loosening stuff in the pan, wondering how they managed to get that bright red-orange color to their sauce. He poured himself a glass of milk, drank it down, then poured himself another. *Okay,* he said to himself.

Behind him, utensils clanked against china as they ate. Nobody said anything to him, but he could feel the anger pouring out of the old man. It blew all around him: go away, go away. *In time,* he answered; ignoring it in the meantime.

Steam came up from the pan, and he scraped some spaghetti into his bowl. He took a deep breath, then carried the bowl, glass and spoon to the table. He pulled out a chair and sat down. Without looking around, he started to eat.

The air in the room got very still, like an iceberg forming all at once. Bullet looked up briefly: his father stared at his plate, his mouth working; his mother stared at the middle of the table, just waiting. Bullet went back to his slow eating.

Finally, his father spoke to him: "At the risk of being repetitive, I said I didn't want to lay eyes on you until you looked like a human being again. I believe you were excused from the table until then." The cold eyes looked right at Bullet.

Bullet looked right back. *The old wind in the old anger,* he thought. He kept his voice quiet when he answered:

"No."

That was everything he had to say about the question, the general question and the particular one.

The old man couldn't do anything, except get up and leave the table himself. "I don't eat with animals," he said to Bullet.

"That's right, you don't," Bullet said.

The only question was how the old man was going to approach this.

"So you're not going to respect my desire not to have to look at you," his father said. He didn't move his eyes from Bullet's face. Bullet didn't need to say anything to that. "Nor my request not to have you at my table."

"It's her table too."

"Abigail?"

She looked at Bullet then, and he couldn't tell what she was thinking. She looked along at her husband, still without expression. She didn't say anything. Bullet heard what that was supposed to say: I'll stand by him as long as we live.

Well, he knew that; he wasn't going to quarrel with either of them about that.

His father chewed on his meat, ignoring both of them. After a long time he said, "I'll take some applesauce."

Bullet dug into the spaghetti again. The old man was just going to pretend it hadn't happened.

"We're out of applesauce."

"You should have told me. I was in town today; you could have done a shopping."

The table they ate at was made of wood, scrubbed down to smoothness. The joints between the separate boards had been made so close that you could see just a thin pencil line where one piece ended and the next began. The table had been put together the same way that fourteen-footer had, somebody's best work. It was as old as the farmhouse.

"I didn't know you were going," she said.

"You should have told me it was time to do a shopping."

She didn't answer.

"There's no call for us to run out of food."

Nobody said anything. Bullet ate. The stuff mushed in his mouth; he couldn't even chew it.

"I didn't know you'd be going into town," she finally answered.

"The fan belt on the tractor is giving out," he told her. "I had to get it replaced."

What was she supposed to say to that?

"And you know I don't enjoy pork without applesauce," the old man said.

I'm sorry, that's what she was supposed to say. The hell with that. Bullet pushed his chair back from the table and went to refill his bowl. Creating a diversion. When he sat down again, he looked at his mother. "This stuff is terrible," he told her. "Want some?"

She shook her head, but her eyes had come alive. "Can you eat this pork chop?" She had one left on her plate.

Before Bullet could answer, the old man announced, "If you don't want it I'll take it. I've got room." When nobody responded right away, he said, "Pass me your plate, there's no need to let it get any colder than it is."

It's almost funny, Bullet thought, ducking his head to hide his expression. He looked sideways at his mother.

"You reap what you sow," his father announced. "Samuel, do you hear me? You reap what you sow."

"I hear you," Bullet answered, without anger. *But I don't have to reap what you've sown, old man.* "Are you thinking about soybeans for the front fields next season then?" he asked.

At his right hand, his mother humphed, the sound of smothered laughter. "You, Bullet," she warned him.

"Okay," he promised her.

The coach read them the letter inviting the team to take part in the state field and track championships, the weekend before Thanksgiving. Twenty-five teams from all over the state were invited. The meets would take place over near Frederick, in the western part of the state, from Friday through Sunday.

"Well, whaddaya think, are you ready?" the coach asked them.

"Sure."

"I'm always ready to miss a couple of days of school."

"I hope," the coach told them, "you're not taking this as lightly as you seem to be. Because that would mean you're seriously underestimating the competition. Only one of the schools we've played this fall is going to be there—Acorn. Remember that meet?"

"The first? They had one coach for every player, didn't they?"

"We're a lot better now."

"Yeah, well, so're they, you can count on that."

That point sobered them.

"And they're the only one of the twenty-five we've gone up against?"

"Look at the list yourselves. We've got no reason to be confident. On the other hand, we do have the element of surprise. They're not expecting us to be as good as we are, not the whole team. Bullet here they know about, but the rest of us. It'll be hard, I'm not trying to kid you. But—I can see it, right out in front of me—" His hand reached out, as if to pluck an invisible cluster of grapes from just overhead. "I can almost touch it. I can almost taste it."

"Hey, Coach, you're not expecting us to *win* this thing, are you? It's only three weeks, we can't get that good in three weeks."

The coach looked deliberately around at the circle of young men. "That would be too much, winning the whole thing. But I'd like to come in among the top ten, and I think this year we just might be able to do that. If you're on your form and you bust your guts . . . I think we're good enough for that. What do you think, are you good enough?"

"How would we know? You're the coach."

"I was planning on being happy just not to be on the bottom again. Like, twenty-second place, or maybe even twenty-third."

"The South," Walker said, "thought it was being invaded by hostile forces. The North thought it was trampling down the vineyards where the grapes of wrath were stored." He gave that a minute to sink in. Long enough for Cheryl to say, "'Battle Hymn of the Republic,' Howe." Walker just looked her in the eye and looked her in the eye.

Bullet smiled to himself. He didn't mind Walker, he decided.

"What do you think?" Walker asked. He waited to hear whatever anybody had to say.

"People were different back then," somebody said, "so we can't think like they did at all."

"What do you mean, different?" Walker asked.

"Well, they really believed in what they were fighting about. The Southerners really believed in their right to own slaves. The Northerners really believed slavery was wrong. To the Southerner, freeing a slave was like . . . giving your dog equal rights, you know? Dressing him up and letting him eat at the table with you."

"You telling me that to prove things are different now?" a black kid asked.

Walker let the wave of laughter ripple over the room before asking another question. "Are people different?"

"People now?" Cheryl asked. "Sure. We know so much more."

"Are you saying that knowledge is the key to progress?" somebody demanded.

"Well, look at the way they used to think war was romantic, dying for your country and all that. They didn't know."

"Just marching along like sheep to the slaughter."

"I guess we *are* really different, Mr. Walker."

"I guess they wish we were the same, don't you think? No draft protesters, no freedom riders? Just followers."

"Wait a minute," Walker said. "Did you know there were riots when Lincoln announced the draft?" Silence greeted this. "And what about John Brown, isn't he the original freedom rider?"

"What are you trying to say?" somebody asked. "That we never learn and just make the same mistakes over and over?"

"History repeats itself," Cheryl said.

"I'll tell you what I think," one of the black girls said. "The South *was* being invaded. No, listen, if—if the Russians put up a fort on Deale Island, wouldn't you think just that?"

"Sabrina's right, we would feel invaded."

"Of course we would, because we'd *be* invaded. Jerk."

"So we'd go trampling down the vineyards, right?"

"Spare me another metaphor."

"Well it's a good one, because it's interesting, because it's so ironic—the grapes of wrath. If you trample the grapes of wrath it should mean you put a stop to war."

"The Civil War was another war to end all wars? But I thought World War I—"

"Which didn't do the job, either. When are people going to learn that making war is not the way to end wars?"

"Yeah! Then what is? Because if you're so smart and know the answer, I wish you'd tell us about it before they send me off to get killed."

"Mr. Walker? What are you getting at?"

Walker had been watching the class. "Ask Mr. Tillerman."

No you don't.

"Ask Bullet? Why? Is he awake?"

Well, that is pretty funny.

"Okay, I'll bite. Bullet? Mr. Tillerman, I mean—what is he getting at?"

Bullet fixed Walker with a glance. The man was looking at him, not het up, not pressuring, not entirely sure of himself; just interested.

"He's talking about the old wind in the old anger again," Bullet said. Not, he could see, what Walker expected him to say. He watched the guy think it through.

"That's pretty subtle," Walker said. "He's right, and he knows it—but I'm here to teach, not mystify. Let's get back to a fact, the draft riots."

They chewed that one around for a while, asking Walker questions about the draft laws at the time, and how much you had to pay someone to go into the army in your place, and what happened to the rioters, and what happened to the draft law. Bullet relaxed back and followed his own thoughts. His father was pushing him out and the draft was out there pressuring him in; how was he supposed to know what he wanted? In one way, getting drafted would be a way of getting away, running free and clear. In another, sticking it out at home would be a way of running beyond the reach of the draft. If he stayed on the farm, that would show his father, show him he couldn't push Bullet out. If he went into the army, enlisted, it would be a way of not being pushed into it. The feeling in the classroom was pretty clear—they wanted to run clear of the draft; not even the draft, really, they wanted to run clear of the danger. But that was one choice they didn't have, because you didn't choose the time you were born in.

Bullet thought on. Although, if it was the old wind in the old anger, the one thing you could be sure of was that it would blow on by. The war would end, his father would die; the wind was going to blow itself by whether you stood firm or ran along, with it or against it. He wondered, his legs stretched out, relaxed, crossed at the ankles, what he was going to decide to do. He had the same feeling he had waiting at the start of a race.

CHAPTER 21

Bullet looked around him. Mountains ringed this long, wide valley. To the east and south, distant mountains were massed shapes across the valley horizon. To the north and west, their shapes were clear because they lay closer. They looked as if some giant lying within the earth had punched out with his fists to form them—rough, strong, irregular, they rose up out of sloping hillsides into stone outcroppings or steep woods. Bullet ignored the crowd of competitors, coaches, officials and judges swarming around him. His eyes were on the mountains and the sky over them. The sky was clear and blue. The early sunlight was starting to take the icy chill out of the air and illuminate the details of mountain faces—here a woods of mixed evergreens and bare branches, there the long vertical gulley formed by spring floods.

It was Friday, the first day, when the schedule was an interlocked network of qualifying rounds. They had arrived last night after a nine-hour bus ride, and now they were standing around with the twenty-four other teams and their coaches, waiting for the day's meets to begin. The coach was wound up tight and so were most of the other people around. Voices swirled all around Bullet. He kept his eyes on the mountains, taking in the look of them where they had been thrust up through the surface of the earth."

"When you're not in a race I want you here, under my eye.

You got that?" the coach told them. They nodded. "Nobody even goes to take a leak without that I know about it," he said.

The qualifying rounds would take all day. Saturday and part of Sunday would be used for the finals. The coach had already warned them that the schedule showed some girls' exhibition matches Sunday morning, and he expected them to show up for those, however they felt. Whether they wanted to sleep in or not, he expected them to be there showing good sportsmanship. Bullet figured, he'd see what he felt like. "You too, Tillerman," the coach had said, fixing him with his eye. Bullet debated saying he'd see, then decided it wasn't worth the hassle. "Okay," he agreed, giving his word.

He had an hour to wait until his qualifying cross-country run. Javelin and high jump were in the afternoon. He let his eyes rove over the milling crowds. Competitors wore shorts and sweatshirts. Everyone else carried clipboards and had whistles hung around their necks. The conversations were punctuated with the sharp sound of somebody blowing on a whistle and the sound of the starter's gun. Bullet stuck around, not talking to anybody, just looking around. Tamer, he noticed, looked relaxed, as he sat talking with a bunch of blacks; most people looked, and acted, nerved up. *Blacks don't get so nervous,* he thought.

Bullet wasn't nerved up. They were running the qualifying cross-country in three different heats, so that the field wouldn't be too crowded. When the time came for his heat, he stood waiting at the start, not looking at anybody, then posed for the gun—and ran.

It was a three-mile course, up and down hills, through forest undergrowth, across deep gullies where little streams trickled, a couple of long, flat stretches along dirt roads, and then, at the end, the quarter-mile flat sprint. Bullet ran it hard. It was a good course, worth putting good work into. It was a strenuous course, because going up and down hills required you to adjust your pace and kept you from steadying down into rhythm except during the straight runs. He came in first, feeling good, feeling worked out, feeling glad he'd had the chance to put his feet down along that course.

The only place he was liable to get into trouble, he thought, on Saturday's five-mile final race, was going to be getting over obstacles. The hurdling technique was designed for level ground. An obstacle on this course would just as likely lead into a downslope or an upslope, and the ground could send you off-balance as you landed. Bullet figured if he fell and took the impact with his arms or chest that would be all right. The danger was, of course, taking the strain on a leg, especially an ankle. As long as his legs were working, he could run. *It'll be a question of how you fall, then, if you fall,* he told himself.

The results came in at the end of dinner. Crisfield had qualified in everything but high jump and the hundred meter. "Somebody pinch me," the coach said, reading off the results as they sat at a long cafeteria table. The college campus where the championships were held had been emptied by its own students for a long weekend. The teams were sleeping in dormitories and eating in the student cafeteria. "How'd we do last year? We stayed in the broad jump and nothing else. Except cross-country. Correct me if I'm wrong." Bullet didn't remember last year. "Tillerman, did you see the time on that guy from Baltimore?"

Bullet hadn't.

"Well, he's gonna give you some competition. He's a runner."

Bullet shrugged and went back to eating. The coach moved on, to encourage the middle-distance runners. Bullet, chewing and swallowing, his mind drifting, let his eyes drift to the westward-facing windows where the last echoes of the setting sun threw the long shadows of mountains down over the valley. He felt a twinge, or something, gearing him up invisibly. *What is it,* he asked himself, *you afraid of a little real competition?* He wasn't sure of the answer.

His mind nibbled at the question through dinner, and especially the next morning during the hours of waiting. He got a sixth in the javelin, better than he would have expected. But he wondered if he was the kind of runner who took winning easy because there had never been any question of whether he would win or not. That kind of jerk.

He looked around at the competitors, as event succeeded event, only one going on at a time now, because these were the finals. The faces were sometimes grimly concentrating, sometimes visibly nervous. But always the bodies were moving, run by an energy that had to come out.

Bullet stood quiet, because he felt that way. He was warmed up, and after lunch he'd jog a little to be fresh and ready. Nobody was allowed to jog over the cross-country course, not for the state finals. That didn't bother him. He looked around, trying to figure out who this Baltimore guy might be, if he would recognize him.

You never had any real competition, he remarked to himself. He felt—not jangled, but jingly; extra alert, physically and mentally. He was always ready for a race, but this was more than usual.

You scared? he asked himself.

I don't think so, I don't think that's it.

Smells like scared to me.

Well it could be; doesn't feel like scared.

How would you know?

I'd know. Scared was what he felt when he first thought maybe he should have brought OD in, to get her to a vet; scared was when he saw how he was making things for his mother.

Scared would be if he found out he was just running to win races easily.

Just imagining that possibility turned the jingles to jangles, and he had an impulse to do a little running in place. *You can't know until you've run the race, jerk. No sense getting het up ahead of time.*

Bullet grinned, relaxed and watched the pole vaulting until his eye—following the arch of a body over the bar—was caught by the clouds blowing in little puffball bunches over the western mountains. They floated high and easy overhead. Behind them, straggling along, came more clouds. Each came into view as it overtopped the mountain, sailing over and onto the clear expanse of sky.

Bullet ate a sandwich a couple of hours before the race, but didn't drink anything. Twenty minutes before the race was to start, he went to join the other competitors. He sat down to do some exercises, to loosen up a little, as the others were doing. The coach came over, said a word to Tamer, who was doing sit-ups, then stood over Bullet. "Run like hell, Tillerman," he said, giving Bullet the thumbs-up signal.

Bullet didn't say anything. *I'm not gonna run like hell, I'm gonna run. Like always.*

Tamer moved over until they were a few yards apart. "I might do okay," he said, doing some slow toe touches. "I watched your heat yesterday—you're a pleasure, Bullet. Regardless of race. Have you seen that guy from Baltimore?"

"Naw." Bullet rested back on his elbows, relaxing down his whole body. The clouds slid by overhead, riding a high wind. He glanced over the rest of the competitors, wondering if he could recognize this runner everybody was talking about. He wondered if physical appearance marked the guy out, if he looked like he was better than the rest. Or if something about the way he was warming up, some confidence, would show. As Bullet's eye roamed over the twenty-odd young men, he saw the pull and stretch of their muscles, the limber movements of arms and legs, the heads bent, concentrating. A couple of times as he looked the field over, he caught someone's eyes on him—they knew who he was. A pair of blue eyes avoided his glance, not wanting to be caught studying him. Bullet came alert and noted the long legs and broad chest of the young man, a good runner's build. Bullet waited: the blue eyes started back to him, but shied away as soon as they saw he was still looking. *That's him.* The guy didn't want Bullet to know he was measuring him. Bullet felt like smiling: maybe he'd go over and introduce himself, make a little conversation, and watch the guy twitch.

As they lined up for the start, Bullet found that he knew where the blue-eyed guy was standing, he found himself aware of the guy's attitude and gestures. *Are you worried he'll beat you?* he asked himself. *I don't know, I don't think so, I hope not,* he answered.

They started from a line. After that, they would run between the crowds for a quarter mile before the pathway narrowed and took off over a hillside. Four and a half miles later, at the finish, there was another broad path, where spectators could see what was happening. There would be check points along the course, where judges were seated unobtrusively, marking times.

Bullet felt his blood dancing along all of the veins and arteries in his body. He breathed in the air, clear and cold from the mountains it had just blown over. He felt good. He felt like running. He glanced over at the blue-eyed guy: *I hope you're as good as they say.*

At the start, Bullet pulled out and ahead. For the first seconds, the first dozen or so sprinting strides, he was aware of the blue-eyed runner. Then he forgot him. And ran.

Over the rise of the first hill, the path twisted down a rocky slope to low brush, then crossed a field abandoned to grass. Bullet sailed over the brush and hit the ground running. He pushed himself, arms relaxed but up and pumping hard, through long grass that swept at his thighs. All of his body was working together for the run, in perfect coordination. His legs thrust down against the ground, his elbows were in tight as his arms pumped easily, his lungs filled with the sweet air and then emptied, and his eyes kept sharp on the marked path ahead, sweeping close, sweeping far, for potholes or burrows, for fences or alterations in terrain or switches of direction. He wasn't thinking, he didn't need to think, because his whole brain was working for him, to judge, to decide, to keep ready.

He went over the scrub growth at the end of the field and into the trees, not cutting his speed at all, even though the branches slapped and scraped at him. At a gulley he stumbled, coming on it too fast, kept his footing about halfway down then went into a roll. He came out of the roll and up into a run up the opposite side. He felt the way his legs pushed him up the steep slope, pushing long, coming down short to push up long again. He used his hands to grab at any branches that came his way and add a little pull to the push.

The course took him up over broad boulders that seemed to be working their way out from under the ground's covering. He leaped down off the far sides of these, choosing to land where more rock showed rather than on leaves. You never knew what was under leaves. The course took him a couple of hundred yards down in a gulley, running its length where there wasn't room on either side of the stream for you to put two feet together, so you were either always straddling the stream as you ran, or running in its icy water with the slippery rocks under your feet. Bullet took the stream, getting fast off every foot so that his forward movement would offset any loss of balance when his feet slipped on the wet rocks. But cold; it was cold.

He clambered up the side of the gulley and registered a judge, a sharp turn a few yards beyond. A good course, he said, not in words but in the quick shifting of his feet at full run to change direction; the toughest course he'd run ever.

Shifting his pace, following the winding path, hurdling over obstacles with his legs ready to take whatever terrain waited on the other side, he ran the course in a celebration. A five-mile celebration. Brain and muscles, bones and will, all worked at the job. Training and talent were both being used, used hard. As he went up the last hill and came down to the level finish, he paced up.

Better than ever before—not just faster, better—he ran the quarter mile. He had seen the crowd gathered there, but they didn't signify except to mark the boundaries of the course. He had no idea whether he was running alone or with a pack of competitors—his senses and brain registered only his own run. The wind roared in his ears, or his blood roared in his ears; something roared in his ears.

Crossing the line and going beyond the crowd before he stopped, Bullet stood facing the mountains. His legs shook and every muscle in his body ached along its long bones. Tired, he was tired—but he wouldn't have minded running that course again.

He stood with the crowd at his back, and the roaring identified itself as cheering and applause. He looked to the mountains, shoved up into the sky. Over their tops, a procession of high-headed clouds raced, gilded by the sunlight.

Oh, yes. Bullet watched the sky. Then he turned around to face the applause.

At the edge of the crowd, moving along to the cement pathway back to the campus, he saw a red blouse. She wore her suit skirt and heels; she wore her hair down her back in a heavy braid.

What's she doing here?

Leaving.

I know, but what—?

He had no impulse to go after her. She was probably in a hurry to catch a bus in Frederick, to return to Crisfield where she would have left Johnny's boat tied up. How had she gotten here at the right time?

He didn't wonder why she had come, even though she'd never come to any meets before, as far as he knew. He knew why she had come. She had wanted him to know whatever it was her being there would tell him, if he saw her. He didn't have to see her, because he already knew it. Now he just knew it more.

And she had wanted to watch him run.

The coach was slapping him on the back, holding out a sweat-shirt for him to put on, calling some numbers into his ear, but Bullet didn't pay any attention to that. He remembered to wonder about the guy from Baltimore, and his attention went back to the course. The coach clapped him on the back and shook his hand and talked. Bullet didn't listen.

The second figure down along the quarter mile finish was the blue-eyed guy, running nicely. Over the line, he collapsed onto the ground, sitting with his head between his knees. His coach massaged at his shoulder muscles with his mouth talking. The blue-eyed guy raised his head and looked around for Bullet. Angry.

Why angry? If he'd run the course like he ran the finish, he'd run well. It was a lovely course to run, smart and tough. *Angry because he didn't win.*

He must have been running to beat out everybody else, which in this case meant Bullet. He must have been in it for the winning. Not Bullet, Bullet was in it for the running. He'd known that before and now he knew it more.

The guy stood up and spat onto the ground. He turned his back to Bullet, knowing Bullet was watching.

Bullet grinned. *He'll learn,* he thought for a second, then corrected himself: *One of those guys who resent mountains because they're taller maybe. Maybe he won't learn, can't.*

A cluster of runners was coming over the approach, and Bullet drifted over to watch. He saw Tamer among them. He saw from the way Tamer was moving that he had run through it and was in control. Along the level finish the group strung out, and Tamer crossed the line second, giving him a fourth in the race.

Bullet watched the rest of that group come in, saw the next reach the descent, then went over to see how Tamer felt.

Tamer had rolled over onto his back, but he wasn't getting up yet. "What a course," he said.

Bullet stood there. "Yeah."

"You like it. I thought it was a killer." Tamer sat up. "Were you terrific? Don't bother to tell me, I know you were—I would have liked to have seen it. Where'd you lose the competition?"

"I don't know," Bullet said.

Tamer laughed, and Bullet grinned at him. "How about you?" he asked.

"I was on his heels for about a mile in the middle there and he didn't like that much." Tamer thought. "It felt good. He's a hurdler, Mr. Baltimore, did you know that? So I'll be seeing him tomorrow. I wouldn't mind beating him myself. What do you think, do you think I can?"

Bullet had no idea.

"He's looking at you," Tamer said, taking a deep, contented breath. "He doesn't care much for you. Me either, it looks like. Tough luck. Bro-ther." He stood up, stretched his arms wide. "Have you taken a look at those clouds? Look at them move. They're something, aren't they?"

"Yeah," Bullet agreed, watching Tamer with regret. Then he looked back to the clouds, once again following their course across the sky.

CHAPTER 22

Sunday's events began at nine, with the hurdles. Bullet got there early, to secure for himself one of the best seats on the course. Overnight, the wind had changed direction and now it blew down the length of the valley from the north. Big, gray-bottomed clouds rode it, like barges. Their bottoms showed flat overhead, but as they floated away you could see white towers rising up from their surfaces.

Bullet sat in the cold air, watching the sky and the mountains, watching the people arrive and arrange themselves on the stands, watching the competitors come onto the track. Tamer had a word with the coach, then did some limbering exercises. Once he was loosened up, he jogged around the course, taking the far outside track so as not to interfere with the hurdles or with the men working and talking at the center.

The oval track, its inner and outer edges lined with white fences, looked more than anything else like a plowed field. The dark cinder paths along which the runners would go were edged with white tape and were the color of newly turned earth. The runners would follow along around those paths, like plowmen, Bullet thought, making the lines other runners would follow. In a way. In a way, everybody was plowing on a track. In a way, everybody was on a track, things put you on a track—your time, your nature, things that happened personally to you, things people did, things you yourself did—and you ran it. You kept to your own path, the markings did that for you, kept you on the path; and the fences inside and outside kept you on the track.

I don't run on the track, Bullet said to himself. *Or really in races.* The high and windy thought frightened him a little, as if he had been blown up among the clouds where he didn't belong. But he didn't belong on any track either. He didn't mind not belonging, that wasn't it. And he wasn't frightened scared. He wasn't even really frightened—it was as if he had just swallowed air too clear, too gold with sunlight, for his lungs. It felt good in his lungs, good beyond any imagining, so good it was frightening. It wasn't his own differences that got to him; he'd always known his own differences. And it wasn't as if he'd really swallowed that cloud high air—he'd just gotten a taste of it. *Wow,* he thought.

The runners went up to their marks. They crouched down into starting position. Tamer had the third inside lane and Mr. Baltimore the fourth. Tamer's head was down but the other guy was looking over across at him, measuring him. The gun went and they took off.

It was clear from the first that the race was between these two. They were both fast, and both took the hurdles smoothly. Tamer had the edge in weight and muscle power; Mr. Baltimore had his length of leg and lighter weight. For the first quarter they stayed together, almost in perfect step.

You're gonna have to run yourself, not him. Bullet wondered if the black could figure that out. He wondered if the black could run his own pace, taking it from nobody else, taking it from himself and forcing it on himself. Physically he could, Bullet knew that. But whether he had the brain and the heart for it, Bullet couldn't be sure. So that—when Tamer's arms came almost imperceptibly up and his stride between the hurdles took him steadily, foot by foot ahead—Bullet sat nodding to himself and smiling in satisfaction. Mr. Baltimore, trying to keep up to Tamer's pace, threw himself slightly out of rhythm and lost a little more distance. Tamer seemed unaware of him as he paced himself up another notch. Because he could do it. *Good for you, Tamer.*

Bullet didn't say anything to Tamer about the race. He figured he didn't need to. Tamer knew what he'd done, and for himself. Bullet didn't go over to join the team members, either, while the first two exhibition events were held. He drifted with the crowd to the ringside to wait through a middle distance run, then stuck around for the high jump exhibition. The sun came out warm whenever it wasn't blocked by clouds. He could feel how sharp the difference in air was on the top of his head, cool shadow and warm light. A dozen girls stood waiting to jump. He was just waiting through the time until the events and ceremonies were over, until they took the long ride back south, until school tomorrow. Next weekend, he'd put in two full days of oystering, and *that* he looked forward to.

She caught his eye first by the stillness of her waiting. She held his eye by her slender height and the proud way she moved into position. The symmetry of her face, the strength of her stride, the calm and concentrated expression of her eyes as brown as velvet: he didn't know if she was beautiful. He only knew her beauty hit him like an explosion. He watched the rhythm and strength of her approach, the high lifting control of her jump and the dancer's grace of her landing. Her shoulders rose—the only acknowledgment of applause. She got into line to wait for her second jump, fell still. Her silky skin shone the color of the black earth where the bay ate away at the marshgrass. *Beautiful.*

The last event of the championships, preceding the presentation luncheon, was the relay race, held in three heats, two elimination and then the final. The coach waved Bullet over to join the team. "How'd you like to be number ten?" he asked.

"Fine," Bullet said.

"I mean, from nowhere to number ten in the state, how does that sound to you, Tillerman?"

Bullet didn't bother repeating himself.

"So I want you to run in the relay. You and Shipp, Johnson and Landry—" He indicated the two blacks who regularly ran the relay.

I don't run on the track.

"If we can just get a sixth in this—and we can't with our regulars—then we'll have the ten-slot. I been figuring out the points. Get ten for sure, and depending on how the rest do in the relays maybe nine. So—will you?"

"No."

The coach was angry. But all he said was, "Shipp, you talk to him."

Tamer's eyebrows flew up. Bullet could have laughed.

"C'mon, guys," the coach said to the other members of the team. "Let's leave them alone to see if anyone can persuade the great man to do something for the rest of us." He shot one last angry and frustrated look at Bullet before leaving.

"No," Bullet said to Tamer.

Tamer unwrapped a piece of gum slowly, put it into his mouth and chewed. Bullet waited.

"So, you don't want to be our token white?" Tamer finally asked.

Bullet grinned. "You got it."

Tamer chewed and thought some more. "The way I figure it, the rest of us can hold them for sure. If you're running anchor then we might do something."

"Sounds about right," Bullet said.

"But you don't run on the track," Tamer added. "And I can't see the other teams being willing to join you out among the fields and flowers."

"Neither can I," Bullet agreed.

Tamer thought and chewed. Bullet waited. The black guy was too smart not to see it, and when he'd given up trying all the possibilities, he'd accept Bullet's decision.

"I have an idea," Tamer said. "Tell me what you think of it. I have an idea that the whole slavery thing was just as bad for whites as it was for blacks. What do you think?"

What?

Bullet shrugged, troubled. "I don't think anything. People are just what they are, and that's not much as a rule."

"That's not what I mean, that's not what I meant a-tall," Tamer pointed out.

"I know what you meant," Bullet snapped.

Tamer waited.

"Nobody can make me," Bullet said, getting angry.

"Brother, even when you're on the track you aren't running on the track, don't you know that yet?"

This time it was Bullet taking time to think. "Okay," Bullet said finally.

"Good," Tamer said, turning away.

"On a deal," Bullet halted him.

"You don't make deals," Tamer said, turning.

"Just this once." Bullet was glad he'd nettled the black guy. "If you'll give me your word to stay out of Vietnam. Don't tell me"—He cut off Tamer's protests—"because you can, you know it. Have another kid. Stay in school. Be a teacher. Get religion, whatever it takes. That one's not your war."

"What, you got a patent on it?"

"You know what I mean."

"How can I give my word about something that has nothing to do with me?"

"Give it. You'll keep it."

Bullet waited.

"Okay," Tamer said. "But I don't know why you feel like you have to get even with me. What difference does it make to you if I figure out what makes you tick."

"You haven't." Bullet denied it.

"Yeah? I told you, brother, I'm a civilized man—I know something about other people. That's what civilization is about."

Bullet walked away, to get his directions for the relay. "You remember how to take the baton?" the coach asked him, still angry, too angry to praise Bullet's good sportsmanship, for which Bullet was grateful.

"I hope so," Bullet said.

On the track, waiting in position, he didn't know what to think of himself for being there. He wasn't at all concerned about how he'd do. How he did had nothing to do with him, however he did. He'd run, that was all. And if they came in among the top three of these teams, he'd have to do the same thing again.

When the baton came into his hand, he sprinted—sudden and fast. It wasn't until he got over the finish line that he learned he'd overtaken two runners to bring them in third. After the second eliminating heat had been held and an exhibition of girls' pole vaulters, they ran the finals.

I can't believe you're doing this, Bullet said to himself, looking around again at the track. But as if his body wanted nothing to do with his opinion, when he felt the baton come into his hand again he took off, running.

The whole team was gathered at the end of that race. Among the incoherent noises, Bullet ascertained that they had again come in third. Hands grabbed Bullet and hoisted him up onto shoulders. "Hey, put me down!" he yelled. Nobody paid any attention to him. They held him on their shoulders, their hands firm on his legs so he couldn't clamber free.

Tamer stood back, watching this, amused. "Let me go!" Bullet demanded. They carried him on around to the starting line. "Put me down, you hear me?" He struggled to get free, but hands reached up to hold him steady. He looked down at all the faces. *All right, have it your way,* he thought, relaxing. After all, he figured they must be feeling pretty good right now, pretty good about him, pretty good about themselves. He wasn't sure how he was feeling, but he was pretty sure about them. And he didn't mind.

They were back at the starting line before he had finally struggled free and gotten his feet back on the ground.

CHAPTER 23

On the twenty-first of March, 1968, Bullet turned eighteen. He officially withdrew from school, first thing. Then he went down to Patrice's. There, drinking coffee and eating a freshly baked roll, he told Patrice what he wanted. "I've got seven hundred dollars and I want to buy the fourteen-footer. With the motor."

"You think I didn't know this? You think there was any other reason for me to paint her red? But I will give her to you, my friend—with the motor."

Bullet shook his head. He took out his wallet and pulled out bills.

Patrice's ugly face looked worried. "I hoped you would let it be a gift."

"It's not for me," Bullet said. "It's for my mother. And—if I buy it for her with money I've earned, then I can really give it to her."

"Well, of course, if that is how you understand it. You won't need the money yourself?"

"In the army? Naw."

"May I ask you a question?"

Bullet shrugged. He slathered butter onto a roll and bit into it, crunching the crust.

"Your hair—or your head—" Patrice started to say.

Bullet laughed. "They're gonna make me grow it."

That amused Patrice.

"One other thing," Bullet said. "There's someone you could hire, if you need someone to work with—"

"You know I need someone. He is a friend?"

Bullet shook his head. "No. I haven't talked to the guy since before Thanksgiving. Not a friend, he's just . . . he's a runner. He's black."

"I am not prejudiced. It is you who are prejudiced, my friend, not I."

Bullet got up to pour himself more coffee. "Not the way I used to be."

"Bring the pot to the table," Patrice told him, then he asked, "How then?"

Bullet shrugged.

"The idea is too speculative?"

"Yeah. Maybe." He did, however, want to try to say it. "You are what you are, and it's what you are that counts."

Patrice couldn't puzzle that out. "But that is no change. That is how you always felt."

"Yeah, but I didn't know it," Bullet admitted. He set the coffeepot on the table and sat down.

"So, you will send this black man to me?"

"I'll give him your name. If he wants to, he'll come talk to you. He can work. He needs a good job."

"This is *not* a good job. There is no future in it, and little amusement."

"It's a good job," Bullet said.

He rode the little boat around and tied it up at the end of the dock, cocking the motor forward to keep the blades out of the water. He didn't know how long it would ride unnoticed there. Nobody had said anything to him about the clumsy cradle he'd built in the barn last December, nor about the way he'd hauled

Johnny's boat up to the barn, dismasted it, stowed the sails under the deck. He had even, knowing that it needed only a rough hand, scraped off the barnacles that the years in the water had grown. Some of them were as big as his thumb.

Bullet jogged up the path through the marsh grass, heading for the house. He almost expected OD to appear out of the grasses, almost turned his head to see her, almost listened for her. It was funny what you remembered.

The old man wasn't in the house at that hour, and his mother was washing the kitchen floor. She used a scrub brush and worked on her hands and knees, her skirt soggy at the hem where it got in her way.

"Momma?"

She wasn't surprised to see him. Her face was quiet as she put the brush back into the bucket, sat back onto her heels and looked at him.

"I'm going."

"I thought so," she said. Her eyes were dark and unreadable, and her voice flat. "Happy birthday. Did you enlist?"

"How'd you know?"

"It makes sense," she said.

He hunkered down until his eyes were level with hers. *Nobody said it wasn't going to hurt.* He was willing to bet it had hurt Liza too. "Listen," he said, "you wanna come with me?"

"What would I do in the army?"

Bullet shrugged. She was right, it would just be another box. It was going to be just another box for him, too, but he'd figured it out. You didn't get out of one box without getting into another, and you didn't get out without it costing you. For himself, he was just looking for a box that fit him. For her—what he was hoping to do was just loosen a board or two for her. It was up to her what she did about that.

Something was squeezing at his heart, and words were strangling in his throat. "I've been thinking," he said. "You remember that birthday party?"

"Eleanor Brown's? I remember. I remember you not wanting to go. I remember driving all the way back along the highway, to pick up the clothes you took off." A reluctant smile moved across her face. "How you got them out of the back of the truck without us noticing, I never knew."

"One at a time," he told her. "I leaned way over, so they wouldn't blow up into view in the mirror."

"And I remember how you looked when we came around to get you out and you were just . . ."

Bullet waited.

". . . bare naked, and laughing . . ." She laughed then, and he joined in.

"Anyway," he said, "I owe you an apology. And Liza, too, because she was looking forward to that party, but she's not around to hear it. I shouldn't have done that."

"Oh, I dunno," his mother said. "It always seemed to me there wasn't anything else you could have done. Being you."

"Yeah," he agreed. She could read him and he could read her. He leaned forward and kissed her cheek.

"So," she said, after a minute, looking at him while he got up, "what can I do for you before you go?"

That was her way of saying good-bye.

His way, he had thought hard about. He knew she wouldn't take the boat, or the hundred dollars he'd left in the top drawer of his bureau for gas and oil—she wouldn't take them just like that, like presents. He knew if he tried to give them to her while he was leaving, that would be hard on her. After he was gone . . . Well, his father would do what he always did, pretend nobody had ever been here, and that would at least be easier on her. But he'd thought about how to make sure she knew he wanted her to have that boat.

"I'm all packed and everything. I've taken everything I want. Whatever I've left behind is for you, okay?" He was thinking of the boat, the hundred dollars—and the farm.

"What would I do with what you've left behind?" she demanded.

"Maybe you'll think of something, maybe not. But it's for you, you hear me?"

"I hear you, boy," she said, getting back to her bucket of water.

His carryall in his hand, Bullet jogged down the driveway. He'd need to find Tamer at lunch, then he'd get the one o'clock bus. The fields stretched away on either side of him, and he stopped at the end of the driveway to look back at them. He'd new-harrowed the fields, and they were ready now to take the crops he wouldn't harvest from them. Tough luck, and he had known what it would cost. But he let his eyes run over them, over the lumpy surface of them. He wanted to keep connected to himself as much as he could; he wanted to be sure he could take with him whatever memory could carry.

DECEMBER 1969

Today, the road all runners come,

Shoulder high we bring you home.

CHAPTER 24

The phone rang, filling the empty rooms with its clamor. She picked it up, and the ringing stopped.

"Abigail Tillerman?" a man's voice asked. "Hello, am I speaking to Abigail Tillerman?"

"You are."

"This is Captain Charles Lockridge, and I'm sorry to tell you that your son, Samuel, has been killed in action."

She didn't say anything.

"Mrs. Tillerman?"

What was she supposed to say?

"We have recovered the body and can send him home to you—"

"No," she said.

"Are you sure?"

"Yes."

"As you wish, of course. I'm calling you myself—he was under my command—because"—and here, for the first time, the voice lost its smooth practiced flow of words—"he was such a fine soldier. A letter will follow, but I was there, and I thought you might want to hear . . ."

He waited for what she would say. She didn't say anything.

"He almost made it, he was coming back, he was running

and they—got him. We were covering him and at first we thought he was just—taking an obstacle, the way he did when he was moving fast but—"

She laid down the receiver beside the phone and walked out of the room. The voice went on talking. She came back into the room with a cleaver in her hand. With the cleaver she sliced through the connection, where the wires came out from the wall. The voice ceased.

She put on a sweater and picked up the phone, putting the receiver back in its cradle to make it easier to carry, coiling the long wire up neatly. She left the house through the back door and made her way down through the barren vegetable garden, between the fields of marsh grasses, to the water. At the end of the dock, the little red boat rode choppy waves. She climbed down into it, lowered the outboard, untied the lines and headed out.

The wind bit at her face and her ears, stung her bare hands. Spray hit her skin, like needles. At the town dock, she looped the line in a clove hitch and climbed up onto the wooden boards. Carrying the phone, she marched up the street to the telephone company. She stood for a minute in front of the big plate-glass window, as if studying the display of telephone models. Behind the display, people sat at desks.

She lifted her hand and heaved the phone into the window. The glass cracked, shattered. Fragments sprayed out into the bitter air—diamond bright, diamond sharp. They flew up and around, like particles of firecrackers exploding.

Abigail Tillerman didn't stand there long. Her chin high, her skirt blown by the wind to tangle her legs, she turned and walked away.

The boat's motor came to immediate life. As she headed out

of the narrow harbor, she thought, *What was that song Liza sang? "The water is wide, I cannot get o'er."* Liza's voice was in her ear, beyond where the motor noise could reach. The wind was behind her now, and the boat bounced along the wave tops. *"The water is wide, I cannot get o'er,"* the voice in her head sang. *"And neither have I wings to fly. Bring me a boat—"* The long, high note lingered.

Well, she had the boat. And the wide water ran, she knew, around the whole world, ringing it around, the encircling oceans that somehow contained and connected all the lands within.

The wind blew at her back, and the wet spume blew onto her shoulders. She lifted her shoulders and squared them, to take up again the burden of long life.